MY DESK AND I

Stories by
K. B. Dixon

INKWATER PRESS

PORTLAND · OREGON
INKWATERPRESS.COM

Cover and interior design by Camille Audelo
Cover illustrations © 2006 JupiterImages Corporation.

The following stories appeared, sometimes in a different form, in the following publications: "Top Drawer" in *V*, "Letters From New York" in *Downtown*, "I Leave a Message" in *Delmar*, "Andrew (A to Z)" in *Make*, "How To Have Your Portrait Painted" in *Hobart*, "Line Drive" in *Open Spaces*, "The Parade" in *The Free Agent*.

www.inkwaterpress.com

Paperback ISBN-10 1-59299-226-9 • ISBN-13 978-1-59299-226-3
Hardback ISBN-10 1-59299-225-0 • ISBN-13 978-1-59299-225-6

Publisher: Inkwater Press

Printed in the U.S.A.

For Sandra Jean

TABLE OF CONTENTS

ACKNOWLEDGMENTS

I would like to thank the magazines and journals in which a number of these stories originally appeared.

I would also like to thank my wife, Sandra—my first reader and my editor.

COFFEE GIRL

How many times have we sat here almost next to each other and not said a word. I don't know. Too many. Please don't mistake my silence for anything other than what it is—which is just me being the way I am at this hour of the day.

*

Yes, I saw you reading the newspaper this morning. How could I not. To be honest with you, I'd have to say that look of concentration struck me as a bit contrived. I could be wrong. Maybe you're as interested in the plight of the Palestinians as you're supposed to be. I was tempted to ask for the sports section but I didn't because I knew you'd recognize the gesture for what it was and think me pathetic.

*

You sip your cappuccino casually but I can tell from the barely detectable twitching of the muscles in your face that you continue to worry about the nature of our relationship and that you are, in fact, worried about this worrying because you think of yourself as someone who is worldly and sophisticated. I don't really think this obsessing is something you object to deep down nearly as

1

much as you claim. I think you object to it, at least in part, because you think I object to it.

*

Today I am wearing my black shirt and my black pants and I can see you are dazzled by my uptown snazziness, but at the same time made uneasy because you were under the impression that we had somehow tacitly agreed to arrive here looking a certain way and I've suddenly arrived looking like this, like someone else completely, and you have not. I can feel you fighting the urge to say something hurtful and sarcastic to me.

*

I noticed you notice me noticing the girl in the magazine ad. You think I am attracted, but I'm not. I mean, yes, she is beautiful and I'm sure some strangely named part of my brain has been stimulated by the sight of her, but I'm more antagonized than aroused. I mean, yes, her hair shines and tumbles fetchingly over her shoulders, and, yes, her eyes are set farther apart than yours, and, yes, she can press her lips together in such a way as to look simultaneously amused and complex—but that attitude of pampered distain she seeks to convey...it completely ruins her for me.

*

I can't explain it but for some reason I have the distinct impression you like the smell of me.

My Desk and I

*

I saw you trying to listen in on that conversation—the one between the girl who always slouches down in her chair and the one with the scary blue fingernails. What did you expect to hear—something about the affair the one who always slouches down in her chair was having with her minty-breathed dentist or something about the one the girl with the scary blue fingernails was having with the pigeon-toed banker who likes to sing Bob Dylan songs in the shower?

*

No, I am not offended by the suggestion that I grow a beard. I've thought about it before but not very seriously because (1) I don't think it would be a very good beard and (2) there would probably be too much red in it. I know you have taken a vote and that several of your friends have agreed with you, but I'm afraid that doesn't really incline me to do it.

*

I can tell by the way you are staring out the window that you're not thinking about me. You're just looking at whatever it is that's going on out there and ignoring it. Funny, it seems such a private moment to have in such a public place.

*

The guy at the cash register is trying his best to be irresistible. He says something to you about it being a small world and it reminds you of what...Disneyland, I think. Any other day you would have followed this recollection—you would have remembered the time when you were visiting and your brother (who always ruined everything for you) got sick and had to be rushed to the hospital with a burst appendix. (You sat in the waiting room picking cotton candy out of your hair while he was being x-rayed. To make the time go by you wrote a postcard home to your dog Boots who was locked up without his ball in your grandparents' dark garage.) But not today...you don't follow this recollection today. Today you let it go where it will. You wash your hands of it. You think instead about your checkbook and its refusal to balance...about your reading glasses, which you must replace because whatshisname, that behemoth from accounting, has dropped his massive briefcase on them.

*

I think you are waiting for someone. You have that look. Who is it? Is it that friend of yours who was arrested for shoplifting shoes—the one who wants to lose weight, clean up her apartment, get a better job, and improve her personality. The one who wears her clothes too tight—whose head squeezes up out of the top of her turtleneck like a dab of toothpaste out of a tube.

*

Do you remember the night I was going to tell you about when it was raining and unpleasant out and I was feeling sort of sick to my stomach so I stayed home listening to the strange noises my refrigerator makes. I listened to them for hours until I sort of put myself into a trance. When I came out of it I felt different, confused—the way you feel when you come home from the ocean.

*

You think I've withdrawn even further into myself than usual today, that I am focusing on some personal peculiarity that I have embraced as being the essence of that which makes me special and knowing. You think it's your job to play along, that I will be charmed by your willingness to champion the unconventional, that we will be knowing and special together. You think it will be amusing to whisper forbidden things.

*

This morning we play some sort of game that involves the making and breaking of eye contact. At the end we have that moment—that frozen, ten-second-thick sliver of forever that's almost Swedish in its enigmatic ambiguity. It hangs there in the air like some fancy special-effects revenant—something that suggests something about whatever it is that's going on between us—a phantasmagorical piñata stuffed with insinuation that we invite our eager chroniclers to attack with flattering interpretations.

*

I don't think you are as unconcerned today as you pretend. The future is not so distant as to feel like never.

MY DESK AND I

I got my old desk back today. I was kicked out of it three months ago. I was called into Steve Kirkland's office one afternoon and told I was being moved to make room for Diana Davis who was being promoted and who just happened to have the prettiest gym-perfected derriere in the department.

The desk I was given was Jim Quinn's. He got kicked out for me. If I were a better person than I am I would have felt worse than I did about this, but there is something wrong with Jim Quinn's life that reminds me of something that's wrong with my own, so the sight of him always irritates me a little and this irritation invariably gets in the way of my feeling as sympathetic towards him as I would like.

Where my old desk was large, flat, heavy, and made of battleship steel, Jim's was bunny-colored, cantilevered, made of some sort of mysterious synthetic extrusion—some cross between wood and plastic. There was a minimalist neatness to it that appealed to my neurotic perfectionist side, but I was never able to form any sort of real attachment to it. I missed my old desk. I missed it a lot.

That missing came to an end this morning when, as part of yet another pointless renovation, we were reunited in this barren new cubicle. I brought a box of stuff with me, but as I look around it's obvious I'm going to have to do some decorating.

Whatever I decide on in the way of doodads, I'm going to have trouble with Tim. Tim's my buddy. He has a bad beard, semi-transparent eyes like a Malamute, and is frittering away his precious, irreplaceable evening hours on something he calls a monograph—a psycho-sociological interpretation of personal office items.

His general thesis is that every non-corporate article in, on, and around one's desk and/or office is a "coded signifier"—an assertion of self, a protest against the annihilating conformity of the corporate environment. Insofar as these protests are invariably of a type tolerated by the corporation protested against, they are not legitimate or real. In other words, they cannot be considered serious. Insofar as they cannot be considered serious, they are, for Tim, things to be disparaged.

While I have an inclination to agree with a lot of what Tim has to say, I don't agree with all of it. Our on-going argument about this particular subject tends to be centered around what I see as the too-exclusive nature of his basic interpretation. Tim thinks everything is a political statement. He doesn't take into account the aesthetic considerations of some displays. He sees all items as some form of protest because he's tin-eyed and can't see them as anything else. Besides, acknowledging such an exception would get in the way of a pretty straightforward diatribe, and Tim, as a zealot, sees the diatribe as the only moral form of discourse.

Tim aside, what I need here are some things that are colorful and convey few, if any, overt messages. (I prefer to avoid earnest exchanges with my co-workers on virtually all the big questions.) Because of my proximity to the telemarketing department, I need things that are dispensable—that is, things I won't miss if they are stolen.

I think after lunch I'll make a quick trip over to Barnes Bookstore. They've got some cheap calendars there and a woman who smells like a pair of leather sandals. (She once sold Bill Clinton a copy of *The Old Man and the Sea*.) Maybe I can find something with photos of France. I like France. I visited there once. I saw the *Mona Lisa* and learned how to eat a ham sandwich on the street. I was a completely different sort of person then.

ANDREW (A TO Z)

a

Arizona. There is a rumor I was born there, but I don't believe it. I don't feel like a person who was born in Arizona, I feel like a person who was born somewhere else—somewhere with trees and an ocean and a liberal political tradition. Somewhere like Washington or Oregon or Massachusetts.

B

Brother. I've never wished I had one and I wonder why. They are supposed to be a good thing to have, but I can't really imagine it. Heather has one. He's fat and depressed and lies around the house all day watching television. I've never met him, but I don't like knowing he is there. I don't like the idea of him rummaging around in the refrigerator.

C

Character. Paul Drabble is one. He is my father's age. He has black hair that he combs back on the sides in a fanciful fashion. At first glance he looks normal enough, but if you peer into his eyes you can tell there are unusual things going on in his head. When you listen to him speak it is like listening to someone doing a translation—instead of from French to English, it is from odd to ordinary. I once played doctor with his daughter—a horsey girl named Anne.

Dog. Janet wants one and I don't. I can barely take care of myself, how am I going to take care of a dog. Janet says she will take care of it and I'm sure she will, but she can't take care of it all the time, which means I'll have to take care of it some, and I don't want to. If I have time to take care of a dog, then I have time to do something else, and if I have time to do something else, I'd rather be doing it because that something else could be *the* something else that makes all the difference.

E

Eschatology. Like most biology professors, my grandfather was inordinately fond of end-of-the-world-as-we-know-it theories. He tinkered obsessively with half a dozen of them—everything from pandemic viral infections to atmospheric aberrations that interfered with basic processes of photosynthesis. He shared them all with me and, as a consequence, seriously undermined my pint-sized faith in the idea that there was going to be a tomorrow.

7

Father. Mine is an insurance salesman by day and an expert on the Kennedy assassination by night. He has written several highly respected articles on the subject—his forte being the debunking of crackpot conspiracy theories. While we have our differences, we share a suspicion of mystery. We fear the uses to which a belief in it can be put.

G

Glasses. When I was nine I hypnotized myself staring at the stars. I wasn't able to snap out of it so I was taken to see a man who may or may not have been a psychologist. All I really remember about him are his glasses—the lenses were thick and tinted an eerie aquarium green.

H

Hearing. I have exceptional hearing so I rely on earplugs most of the day. I wear them when Patrick, the guy in the office next to me, is playing his hideous radio or being visited by his friend Teresa who sounds like a 150-pound macaw. I wear them in the evening at home when I read, when I draw, when I sleep. I never go anywhere without a pair because I never know when I am going to need to shut something out. The ones I am using now are orange and made of silicon. They are the highest-rated reusable earplugs currently made anywhere in the world. It says so on the box.

I

Isolation. There are people who believe I need to be rescued from it. I suppose it's no surprise that I'm not one of them.

J

Jealous. I am sure I am more so than I know, but she has never given me reason to find out. I've grown sort of accustomed to this certainty over time, but in the beginning it amazed me that she did not seem to realize how much more she deserved.

K

Kafka. I remember reading a small red paperback copy of *The Trial* and liking it very much—thinking what a luxury it was to feel persecuted. It was so much better than feeling simply ignored.

L

Lights. She leaves them on and it drives me crazy. There is the waste, which disturbs me on several levels. And there is the fact that when one burns out I will have to go next door and borrow Doug's ladder because our ceilings are so fashionably high I can't get to them with my sad little stepstool. Doug is one of those easygoing people with large wrists. He will be happy to loan me the ladder, but before he does he will have to tell me about the last time he used it.

Mother. She is a gaunt woman with strange ideas about nutrition. She is obsessed with vegetables—broccoli in particular. Apparently if you eat enough of it you will live forever and have beautiful skin.

n

Nickname. His is Chuckles. It's ironic. A disgruntled, pot-bellied loner with an interest in guns, I expect him to come in here one day and start shooting people. I've been tempted to express my concerns formally, in writing, so that when it happens there will be a paper trail for my family's lawyers to follow.

O

Office. Mine is small and gray and one and a half floors away from my supervising department. I've got two phones, a computer, a fax machine, a printer, an adding machine, a photocopier, two file cabinets, a stapler, a scraggly dieffenbachia, and a clock.

P

Party. It's Daniel's 40th birthday party. I don't really know him, but Janet does. She likes him. (She likes everyone.) She has worked with him in the past and been on a committee with him and feels sort of obligated to be here. She didn't want to go by herself so she asked me and I had to say yes because we made a bargain long ago about evenings like these, and she was holding me to it.

Q

Quality. This is Janet's theory of clothes: quality rather than quantity. I agree, which is why I guess I sort of have a look. I don't own much, but what I do have tends to be good and go together. With minor variations, my ensembles get repeated frequently. There's my duffel coat with my cords, my bomber jacket with my khakis, my parka with my jeans.

Reading. As a rule, I don't much like to be read to myself. This hasn't stopped me from going to things called "Readings," however (though I'm more likely to try something called "Arts and Lectures Series" or "An Evening with So and So"). Whatever it's called, if I am there, I am hoping the reading part will be minimal or nonexistent. What I want is to hear the writer talk extemporaneously about whatever it is he or she wants to talk about and to answer questions. But, of course, questions can be a problem. They are almost never any good. If you have been to entertainments like this before you know what I'm talking about. Too many get asked by people trying to sound "literary" who just bore the bejesus out of you with some long-winded thing about the aesthetics of the unreliable narrator. I like the ones that get the writer off on some barely-related tangent. Tangents are the sunshine of evenings like these.

S

Sister. Technically I have two, but practically it's more like one and an eighth. The second was born when I was fourteen and I have not seen her since I left home for college. She survives in my life mostly as a name—someone to whom I must send a Christmas card.

T

Tired. I am tired all the time. I'm tired when I go to bed. I'm tired when I get up. I'm tired in the middle of the day. Something is wearing me out. I think I know what it is.

U

User. It's entirely possible that there are too few intravenous drug users in my life—at least that's the feeling I get from Stephen who has a life full of them. According to him, if you are not personally acquainted with someone who's in prison for murder, then you are not leading a vital, authentic life. If your girlfriend hasn't burned you with a cigarette or stabbed you in the buttocks with a pen knife, then you are not living at the white-hot center of it as you should. But then, of course, Stephen is a romantic.

V

Vendetta. I don't know what his name is, but he is taller than I like people to be and married to a woman who is much younger than he is. He parks his spectacularly ugly blue car in front of my house and leaves it there where I have to look at it every day. I have left notes on his windshield asking him to please move the thing occasionally so I could look at something else once in a while, something less forlorn, but he has not responded. A week ago I emptied a jar of honey on his hood.

W

Wine. I had a glass after work with egg-shaped John. It was a pinot noir from California. It was good, but nothing exceptional—still John wanted to talk about it. He wanted to discuss its plumminess, its relation to the great vintages, its structure, its concentrated black-fruit flavors, its glycerin levels. He is one of those people who is not smart but who is desperate to seem smart, so he specializes. Besides wine, he knows way too much about Gustav Mahler.

X

Xenophobia. I'm afraid of what strangers will want from me so I avoid them as much as I can. I have been avoiding them more lately than I used to, and I hope to avoid them even more in the future—if Janet will let me.

Y

Years. I like the even-numbered ones. It has something to do with a deep-seated love of symmetry.

Z

Zorro. When I was six I wanted to be Zorro. I had the hat, the mask, the cape. I also had a small plastic sword tipped with a piece of chalk so I could put my mark on things. I have a picture somewhere of me in full regalia. I'm standing in our livingroom with my friend Dexter. Dexter is dressed as a sailor. He has an arrow through his head.

I LEAVE A MESSAGE
(Variations on a Theme by Lydia Davis)

I call and leave a message because I just don't want to see her tonight. There are nights like that, when I don't want to see her—partly because I am who I am and partly because she is who she is. Lately it's been more because she is who she is than because I am who I am, but I can't tell her that because she is who she is and if I told her that she would react in that way she has and before you knew it we would be up to our yahootie minutens in yet another crisis, a crisis that would require days and days of the most arduous, arcane, complicated, impossibly nuanced negotiations to resolve.

The message I leave is that I am going to be busy, that I have a "thing," that I will call her later. I know I should be more specific, that I should define "thing" in concrete terms, that in not doing so I am antagonizing her, but I don't because I am tired and sort of depressed and this is my sad way of lashing out, of expressing my frustration with the demands that are being made of me, demands that I explain myself even when I need not to—especially when I need not to.

She will wait some unspecified amount of time after she gets this message before she calls, and when I do not answer, she will wait again. And call again. And when I do not answer again, she will get in her car and drive over here. I can't tell you how many times she has done this in the past. She will cruise slowly up and down the street, seeing again and again that the lights are not on in my apartment. Eventually she will stop and come up and try to look through the curtains. She will knock on the door and when I do not answer she will leave me a note, a carefully worded note, that suggests I am driving her to extremes, that I am torturing her, that I know how she is and yet I continue to treat her the way I treat her—being busy and having "things"—that I am heartless and unwilling to allow her the least bit of authority in this relationship and that in this I may serve as a simple, emblematic symbol of my gender.

When she gets back home, she will call again. I will not answer. She will call again. I will not answer. She will call a third time and let the phone ring and ring and ring, and finally I will answer because I just can't continue not to. She will want to know where I have been, and I will tell her out to the movies. She will want to know why I was letting the phone ring, and I will say that I had no idea I was letting it ring, that I just came in the front door, and I will try to sound like I am a little out of breath from having hurried to pick up. She will ask if I got her note, and I will say yes I got it, but I hadn't read it yet because I was rushing in to get the phone. She will say don't read it, just throw it away, and I will say okay, and she will want to know if I would do that, not read it, just throw it away, and I won't know what to answer, and I will say that because I have gotten tired of trying to guess the right answer to these questions—I have, in fact, come to believe there is no guessing right, there is only guessing wrong.

She will ask why I didn't tell her I was going to the movies, and I will say, unconvincingly, that I don't know because I don't want to try to explain about not wanting to explain because—well, I don't want to explain, and I have a distinct sense that trying to explain about not wanting to would do nothing but provide opportunities for purposeful misunderstandings.

She will want to know who I went to this movie with, and I will make up someone from work. I will call him Steve. She will want to know what movie we saw, and I will name one that I know at least a little something about. She will ask me what I thought of it, and I will tell her it wasn't very good in the vain hope that she won't go out and see it and ask me more detailed questions later. Of course, she won't believe me. No matter how hard I try, the whole thing will sound wrong. I don't have any friends at work who I would go out to the movies with on the spur of the moment. I don't have any friends at work period. What I'm telling her is not true, and she knows it. (If it were true, it would signify something new, something she would need to get to the bottom of. We must always be getting to the bottom of something—if we are not, we have to get to the bottom of why not).

She will choose to believe that something is going on and that that something has something to do with another woman. This will surprise me a little because knowing her as I do, I have always felt—in this respect anyway—she knew me, knew that whatever else was going on, it would never be another woman because, whatever else was going on, I would never have the energy for another woman; but if she does know this, she will choose to ignore it in favor of the cliché because the cliché is so much more interesting.

We will argue for what seems to me forever—until, in exasperation at my clearly flagging interest in covering the same ground yet one more time, she hangs up.

She will wait some unspecified amount of time before she calls back, and when I do not answer, she will wait again. And call again. And when I do not answer again, she will get in her car and drive back over here. It will be late, long past the time when we both should be in bed asleep, but she prefers this sort of thing go on all night because if this sort of thing doesn't go on all night, it can't really be this sort of thing—it has to be some other sort of thing, something less.

She will knock in that special sad, tragic, defeated way she has—three boneless, carefully calibrated, ennui-ridden raps somewhere up just above mid-door. I won't really want to put my arms around her, but I will because she will look so miserable and unhappy. She will be quiet, expecting me to say what she is expecting me to say—namely, that it is over between us. But I won't say this—I won't say it is over between us because while it is over (in some way), I can't say it is because saying it is will not really make it so—saying it is will only start making it so, and I don't want to start making it so because I am not anywhere near the emotional place I would have to be in to do that.

We will sit on the couch holding hands and talk for hours about why we can't keep doing what we have been doing. We will talk about what doing what we have been doing is doing to our relationship and how that relationship—which has had this done to it over and over again—has changed, and probably not for the better. We will become grandly theoretical, making abstract points about abstract points about abstract points which, in their per-egrinations—turning, turning in a widening gyre—take on strange, polysyllabic lives of their own.

She will outlast me, of course. She has a genius for this sort of thing and is indefatigable. I will be tired and the time will come, as it always does, when my only interest in the conversation will be in finding a way to end it. I know it will not end until she is convinced that things have been made right between us once again, and that I will not be able to convince her they have been made right between us once again until I convince myself, so I will set about doing this—convincing myself and conse-quently her—as completely as I can. I will apologize, ad-mitting that I have not been up to the task of being who I should. I will take back whatever needs to be taken back, and I will acknowledge that, when properly looked at, all sorts of things have been just the opposite of what I had thought or suggested. If lately there have been nights like this, nights when I did not want to see her, it will be more because I am who I am than because she is who she is. It will be my selfishness and not her neediness that is jeopardizing our perpetually jeopardized relationship. I will say that I am sorry.

We will talk about being all right for awhile, and with the sun starting to come up, the sky getting creamy, she will get into her small, square car and drive off. On her way home she will replay the entire evening. She will have most of the conversations over again, verbatim, and she will become uneasy. She will start to doubt what she had let herself believe, and she will become desperate for some conclusions. She will want to know how much we are what she thinks we are and how much we are something else. And if we are something else, she will want to know what it is, and if it is what she is afraid it could be, she will want to know if there is anything she can do about it.

She will call me at work to see how I am. I will say I am tired, and she will say she is sorry and that she wants to see me so we can talk over what it is we have just gone through. I will say I'm not really up for talking over what it is we have just gone through, that I am exhausted and that I am going home and going to bed. She will say she wants to go home and go to bed with me, and the way she will say this will break my heart, and I will say okay. I am who I am and she is who she is, and if we are not who we were, we are who we are, and whoever that is, whatever that is, it is something and not nothing, and as something, it may not be enough, but it is not not enough either, and a distillate of our predicament is hidden in that nest of negatives.

TWENTY-EIGHT DAYS

1

I remember reading a strange little book once that spent a number of pages describing men's-room behavior in minute detail—the noises, the odors, the competitive urination. As I recall, there was a focus on the whistling phenomenon—the way whistled tunes got passed around like viruses. There is not much whistling here. Certainly not enough to make a big deal about. Maybe it's a dying art. Hope so. (Note to self: Look into psychology of whistling—who, where, why?)

2

Three calls from upstairs today. That's three more than I would like to get. Calls from up there are never a good thing. They tend to be either accusations of wrongdoing or requests for services I'd rather not provide. In this case all three were of the accusatory variety and, for a change, wrongly so. Even though I explained myself satisfactorily to the inquiring minds who wanted to know, I'm still not happy. Contact with management just uglies up a day and there's nothing you can do about it.

3

Periodically I come in thinking I am going to have a better attitude about this job, and I do—for about 30 minutes. After that my old attitude sneaks up on me and before I know it I'm back to my old ways—avoiding everyone, watching the clock, hiding in here.

4

Carl just walked by. I always wonder about him. Old, frail, ugly, gay, poor, and of average intelligence—what makes him happy? How does he get from one day to the next? (Note to self: Forget about Carl. The more you think about him, the more likely it is you'll throw yourself in front of a train.)

5

Michelle is always wanting to share some story about someone in her family who did something or other and I have to sit here listening and looking deeply interested when all I really want is for her to stop talking to me and go away so I can get back to doing whatever it is I was doing before she stopped by. I am always afraid that somehow it's obvious that this is what I want, that whoever it is I'm talking to knows what I'm thinking, that it's written all over my face, given away by all sorts of involuntary flickers and twitches, so I try extra hard to have a sincerely engaged expression because as much as I want her to go away, I don't want to hurt her feelings.

6

New driver's license today. The photo was shocking.
They're always bad, but this one is the baddest ever.
I look like my grandfather. I've got two chins, a funny
neck, and the flash has turned my mustache completely
gray. It's useless as I.D.—or at least I hope it is.

7

I am not looking forward to going through the getting-to-
know-you stuff with the new guy Gary. He is replacing
Donna who I worked with for four years and who is leaving to go to dental school. While he is an inherently more
entertaining person than Donna—more thoughtful, more
interested in things—he is also more difficult because he
is older, slobbier, stranger, and more set in his ways. It's
going to take weeks, maybe months, to figure out just
exactly what it is we want to talk about, what it is we
want to joke about, who it is we want to hate, how much
(or how little) of our private lives we want to share, how
much silence we can allow (or demand).

8

I'm allergic to whatever it is that blooms earliest in
spring. My eyes start to itch. My nose runs. I can't sleep.
I take over-the-counter antihistamines, but I don't like
them very much. They do what they're supposed to do
with regard to my symptoms, but they make me feel

funny—which means from the end of February to the middle of April I'm not quite myself. The sad thing is, during this time I'm not quite anybody else either.

9

I barely know her but still she tells me in detail about her dying dog—about its lumps and tumors and gastrointestinal misfortunes. I'm sorry for the dog, but I refuse to be sorry for her—at least not as sorry for her as she wants me to be. I'm not handing over my sympathy because she demands it. Just because I know her name doesn't mean I owe her special space in my head.

10

I always get a little tense on haircut day. I don't like being fiddled with, and I don't like getting home late. Bob, the guy who cuts my hair now, is better than Brenda. He doesn't fuss as much, and he's faster. He doesn't smell as good as Brenda did, and he has hairy forearms that tickle the sides of my face when he's cutting the stuff on top, but he's better with the small talk. He doesn't make me work as hard, and he doesn't seem inclined to want a "relationship" with me. (Note to self: Consider again a simpler, more politically ambiguous hairstyle.)

11

I'm pretty sure his name is Chris. He's a nice guy. I like

him, but he has this need to make a certain kind of impression on me and it's distracting. Why is it so important? It shouldn't be. I'd be much more likely to have the impression he wants me to have if he weren't trying so hard to make it.

12

Don is an odd sort of person—like Glenda. Her sort of oddness I understand. His I don't. He has a beard, a boat, a wife, and a niece with some sort of condition that causes her to periodically pass out when she gets too excited. Last weekend he built a replica of the Pittock Mansion out of popsicle sticks.

13

As a rule I have a tendency to be in favor of moderation—except when it comes to temperature. Sixty degrees, like it is today, is roughly speaking the climatic equivalent of the middle way. It's bland—like modesty. It's probably my least favorite temperature. It's neither stimulating nor stupefying. It's blah—like chicken broth.

14

As expected, Drew was the first one in the office to make a comment about bewaring the Ides of March. There's nothing like a preening allusion to the excellence of one's secondary education to start the day.

15

His name is Greg. He looks a little like a squirrel. He is the owner of the saddest sandwich I have ever seen—a flat, plastic-bagged, centerless, two-pieces-of-brown-bread thing. He's one of those people who depress you because they require so little of life.

16

I had a dream last night. In it my name was James. It was like I was a character in a short story, a father—one of those who is a little more fatherly than the average father you find in everyday life; one of those with a fatherly haircut and a cleft chin; one of those who wakes up in the middle of the night with his pajamas soaked in sweat, his heart pounding, terrified his daughter has been kidnapped by the worst sort of person he can imagine—someone with no known address; someone stalky and hairy and smelly; someone with stubby fingers and hideous intentions. One of those fathers who jumps up and rushes across the hall to check on his little girl. There she is. Her name is Lindsay. She's eight and beautiful—a daughter made up of the best parts of other people's daughters (Mark's, Bill's, David's)—the daughter I would have if I could have the daughter I wanted. There she is, curled up like a cat, asleep under her favorite fuzzy blanket.

17

When I walk Janet home it will be later than I would like it to be. I will want to come up, but because she is a responsible person who cares about her job and has to get up early to go to work, she won't let me. I will leave her at the door with a kiss and head off dejectedly down Taylor. By the time I get to 19ᵗʰ I'll be thinking about Mrs. Montgomery again, wondering if she has tried anything while I've been away. But mostly I'll be thinking again about Dr. Chirgwin, about his sing-songy salesman's voice, his prescription pad, his self-serving inclination to see me as someone determined to fail. I'll wonder who's the best me he will think I can be. Who would that me be having dinner with on a night like this? Who would that me be taking to the movies? Who would that me be wishing something better for than the best he could wish for anyone?

18

I have a grudging admiration for Brian. He's been fired from at least four jobs and seems sublimely unphased. His belief that there will always be something else, that things will work out, seems remarkable to me. I'll never understand how people can believe some of the things they believe. I envy them both their carelessness and their certainty. (Note to self: Rewrite resume.)

19

The wind today ruined my last good umbrella—the black, telescoping one with the hooked handle. I can't replace it because for some reason the people who used to make it have stopped making it, and so far as I can tell, nobody else has started. I'm going to have to move to a different style, one with a straight, knob-like handle. I can tell you right now I am never going to like it as much.

20

Patrick is looking for me. He wants to talk about my joining his "team." I don't want to join his team. It's just a larger, more conspicuous, more odious version of the team I am already on. I will try to avoid him until I can come up with some sort of diplomatic demur, but this is a tricky business. One wrong thing said and there will be months of gratuitous supervision.

21

It is that time of year. I am starting to see people around who I would rather not see. People washing their cars, digging in their yards, pushing their children around on tricycles.

22

I'm having trouble exercising. I've been doing sit-ups, push-ups, and deep knee bends for some time now, but lately I find myself being lured away from my regimen by the pleasures of the bottle. Is this a sign that I've started to concede something? As I have fewer and fewer days left to me the idea of seizing them has gotten more attractive. If no one comes to the end wishing they'd spent more time at the office, neither do they come to it wishing they'd done one more set of jumping jacks.

23

There are jobs that are worse than this one. Lots of them. Lots of them that are lots worse. It makes me feel spoiled and pathetic to be so unhappy. What do I think I'm owed?

24

Every time Neil comes back from vacation he stops by my desk and says something to me about the current state of world affairs. He doesn't really know much about the current state of world affairs, but he thinks I do because from time to time I'll pass on jokes I've picked up. As a point of contact it isn't much—but it seems enough for us.

25

I'm giving up tuna fish sandwiches. I don't like the way they make the office smell, and I'm worried about mercury poisoning. I already have headaches, mood swings, memory loss, and trouble concentrating. Why make matters worse?

26

I like being in the woods for about an hour. I used to

like being in them longer, but something has happened to me. Julie is a little frightened of them; she thinks they're creepy. She made her husband promise never to take her into them unless absolutely necessary. I suspect she imagines them to be filled with one or another sort of goblin. I find them soothing and significant—a place to find perspective. But I am only interested in being soothed or placed into a larger context for a short time. I get bored even though I know I'm not supposed to. After I've breathed the air, listened to the sound of nothing, and had lunch on a flat rock, I'm done. (Note to self: See if I can re-read *Walden*.)

27

I bought another book about mathematics and I can't say why exactly. I don't have a mathematical bone in my body, but there's something about these strange arguments I find irresistible. It feels like a way for me to run my thumb along the edge of something.

28

I love three o'clock because the end of the day is in sight. I can relax and stop searching for ways to make the time pass. I can feel my life, the one I truly live, waiting for me out there. We will soon be reunited. (Note to self: Get new battery for my watch.)

HOW TO HAVE YOUR PORTRAIT PAINTED

First find a painter. It's not as easy as you might think. Ask your artist friends if they know anyone. They won't be offended that you haven't asked them—they are abstractionists and performance whatnots and clearly dozens of isms beyond this sort of thing. Be persistent. Eventually someone will admit to knowing someone who will admit to knowing someone who will admit to knowing a figurative painter. Get this painter's name. Talk to him. His political opinions will be appalling—the neanderthalic excrescencies of talk-radio—but his artistic judgments astute. Visit his new show.

*

The gallery where this show is opening sits just off a covered courtyard on one of the local community college's more distant campuses. It's a small rectangular thing roughly the size of your kitchen. Pass on the punch they offer at the door and don't be put off by the places lack of grandeur. There will be a crowd of chit-chatty arty types. Ignore them as graciously as you can. Tumble around the periphery of the exhibition—like a heavy thing in the clothes dryer. Look at the pictures. Tally the yes-I-like-thats and the no-I-don'ts. Keep an eye out for something special—something like the one titled *Rachael* (a sad-looking woman with long, tangled black hair). Ask yourself if this is something you really want to do. Ask yourself if this is something you can accommodate psychologically.

*

Spend a week talking yourself into it. You were brought up on the romantic idea of the artist as hero, as visionary, as genius who peers through the veil of mere appearance to see the Truth. Get over it. Don't worry about the painter discovering and displaying something you do not want discovered and displayed. If you want to worry about something, worry about the painter imposing something—either inadvertently or for his own sinister painterly purposes.

For example, look at Velasquez's famous (and frightening) portrait of Pope Innocent X. Study it even cursorily and you will have an impression of who this Pope was (and, consequently, who he was not). For instance, it's not likely you would conclude this was a man with a sense of humor. But what if he did have a sense of humor? What if that was one of his most salient features? What if that was how he knew himself and was known by others? What if Velasquez painted him the way he did to make a point (iconographically) about what he felt to be a certain mercilessness at the heart of contemporary ecclesiastical law?

*

Meet the painter for a cup of coffee. Wear a corduroy

coat. There are some things you need to discuss. To begin with, of course, you want to know how much this picture is going to cost.

You also want to know how long it is going to take to complete. You are a busy person with neither the time nor the inclination to get involved in a protracted project, and the literature of portrait painting is filled with stories of marathon encounters. There are Lord's 18 sittings for Giacometti, Vollard's 115 for Cezanne, and West's 300+ for Auerbach. When the painter tells you one, maybe two sittings, feel encouraged—sort of.

I say sort of because, while this is the answer you want to hear, it is not—you realize when you hear it—a piece of completely comforting news. It confirms what the pictures themselves have suggested: this is a painter who is to some degree committed to the aesthetic of the spontaneous. While there are lots of things you like about these sorts of pictures—the sort that are the product of painters who are to some degree committed to the aesthetic of the spontaneous—there are a couple of things about the idealization of the impulse that trouble you. One is the anti-intellectual nature of this idealization, the other is a certain sanctimoniousness at the heart of the cult—the feeling that the spontaneous, predominantly unmediated response to certain visual sensations captures some sort of primal authenticity that lends the resulting picture a certain sort of superior moral authority.

*

You have a couple of special requests. Don't feel bad about them. Before the artist was a hero who saw through the veil of mere appearance to the Truth, he was a craftsman and, as such, usually worked to order. Patrons would write up elaborate contracts stipulating all sorts of things from the amount of a certain shade of blue to be used to the number of winged cherubs to be seen circling granddaddy's head. After he became a hero who saw through the veil of mere appearance to the Truth, these formalized entreaties came to be seen as gross and impertinent intrusions. Your entreaties are neither gross nor impertinent. They are discreet and reasonable and in no way interfere with the integrity of the work, so ask away. Show your sensitivity to the issue by using a supplicant's tone.

Ask first for something smaller. You are afraid you are going to hate it, and the smaller it is, the easier it will be to hide. Explain the request is predicated on one of necessity's unfortunate dictates—your apartment is tiny and many-windowed, and you just don't have much in the way of good old-fashioned wall space.

Secondly, ask for something darker. Most of the pictures in the show were done in a bright, quasi-Matissian pallet of reds, oranges, and pinks—a pallet to which you do not respond. Ask for something closer to the depressive Flemish end of the spectrum—something maybe in blacks and browns. (You have seen slides of other work done in these more subdued tones, so you know this is not something to which the painter has essential objections.)

Make a commitment. Wave goodbye to any illusions of humility.

*

My Desk and I

Your first sitting is in the artist's kitchen. He is building a small studio onto his house. He thinks it will be usable even unfinished, but it isn't so you end up seated across from each other at the breakfast table. To begin, he draws a couple of quick sketches of your head. When he has the lumps and bumps of your lumpy and bumpy physiognomy sorted out, he picks up a canvas, props it against the table, and starts to work. (You will discover later how uncongenial this is for him. When you get into the studio on your second sitting you can see he prefers to stand and move around when he works. In fact, at times he appears to dance.)

In all, the picture will take three sittings. At first you talk about art—real art, big-name art. (You are variously prepared: you have your subscriptions, your copy of Gombrich, your black turtlenecks. And the artist—in his dreary, workaday, bringing-home-the-bacon life—is a teacher, an uncommonly good and well-read one.) You talk about Rembrandt's command of light and shade, Rubens's symphonic qualities, Ribera's debt to Caravaggio. On your way home that evening it will occur to you that in chewing all this highfalutin fat you may have made the painter nervous, bedeviling him with concerns about the nature of your expectations. At the next sitting you try to lighten things up. Bring something you doodled at lunch. It's titled "An Artist's Alphabet": D is for Dada, the movement that was, in a sense, MOMA's papa; E is for Easel, the rack on which an artist's hopes are tortured; F is for Form, the shape ships are in; L is for Line, the graphic rope an artist throws around an idea; M is for Marble, the rock of ages; P is for Perspective, something we no longer have; R is for Right Angle, the turn Mondrian took on his way to Neo-Plasticism; T is for Theory, the last refuge of a scoundrel; W is for Wallpaper, the works of Barnett Newman; X is for Xerography, the sincerest form of flattery; Z is for Zeitgeist, the way the wind is blowing according to the editors of *ArtForum*.

*

When the picture is finished, take it home wrapped in butcher paper like a pork chop. Sitters' reactions to their portraits have run the gamut. Gertrude Stein loved Picasso's picture of her—it became the centerpiece of her famous salon. Winston Churchill hated Graham Sutherlin's. He said it made him look like he was having a difficult stool. He had it destroyed. Manet took a pair of scissors to a picture Degas did of him and his wife. You have no idea what your reaction is going to be, but whatever it's going to be, you are determined it's going to be had in private.

When, sequestered in your living room (glass of wine in hand), you see the picture for the first time, feel tremendous relief. Exhale. The sensation is a little like hearing from your doctor that certain test results have come back negative. Whatever else it might be, it is first and foremost "good." In this regard, it's not something you are going to have to be equivocal about. That threshold hurdle cleared, start looking for your features. Likeness—while not a high priority—is not entirely unimportant. Get excited when you find your nose, your chin, your eyes.

You have no idea what you expected, so you have no idea how close this has come to being it. Over the next few days relax into an acceptance of it being whatever it is. Assess it on its own terms. Keep looking at it. Keep wondering if it is you. Show it to someone else. Ask: is it me, does it challenge one's sense of the familiar, further the debate about volumes and voids, seem Kokoschkafied, allude to an underlying melancholy?

Show the picture to your mother when she comes to visit. She likes it. Mention this to the painter. He will be pleased. Mothers, he will say, are a tough audience.

*

Live with the picture for a while. Say a year. Congratulate yourself on having gone through the experience. Ridicule acquaintances who seem fearful of trying it themselves. Call them lily-livered. Write about the experience for one of your favorite publications. Borrow a literary device from you know who.

LETTERS FROM NEW YORK

Dear Alex,

If I could bring myself to use an exclamation point, this would be the time to do it. I am here!—New York. The Big Apple. If I get up really close to the window in our hotel room and look out sharply to the right, I can see a honey-colored sliver of the Empire State Building. From the rooftop it's nothing but landmarks.

This afternoon we took the train out to Flushing to watch the Mets play the Cards. In the middle of the pre-game announcements there was a request that we report any incidences of "antisocial behavior" to the nearest usher. This sort of caught me by surprise. Being antisocial isn't something I expected a New Yorker to notice, let alone object to.

Tonight we are going to a nice little trattoria in Greenwich Village—a neighborhood legend—Ennio & Michael's.

Dear Doug,

Taking into account your inexplicable love of all things colonial, I thought I'd tell you I just had lunch on the steps of Federal Hall. I sat on the very spot where George Washington was inaugurated President in 1789. I can't say this fact lent any special spice to my gyros, but perhaps I just don't have the right sort of imagination.

There is a bronze statue here by John Mood commemorating the inauguration. George is standing with his hand extended—presumably as it was when he took the oath of office. To me it looked like he was asking us to quiet down.

Dear Tom,

We visited the New York Public Library this morning. We wanted to see the marble lions out front, the third-floor reading room, and Bryant Park—home of the demented and drug dependent. The lions were all we managed. The library was closed, and the park—where they are now building—was surrounded by a chain-link fence. (On the 42nd Street side it sports a sign that reads: "Littering is filthy and selfish, don't do it.")

Robert Benchley once wrote a piece titled "So You're Going to New York," telling tourists that when it came to visiting points of interest in the city, they were as likely as not to find them torn down or closed. He wrote this in 1929. Some things never change.

In addition to the library and Bryant Park, here is a list of things we have found closed so far:

1. Backstage on Broadway Tour
2. Leo Castelli Gallery
3. Lutece's
4. Elaine's for lunch
5. The Rose Room at the Algonquin
6. Lou Singer's Ethnic Tour of Brooklyn
7. Angelina's

And we've only been here two days.

Dear Sue,

We are not dead yet. And please don't worry. It doesn't look like we are going to be killed any time soon.

The day before we left I noticed a letter in the paper about Portland's crime problem. New York was held up as an example of what can happen if the sort of things that are going on in Portland now aren't remedied pretty soon. The correspondent said that New York was a frightening mess—in fact, he said, if one hadn't lived there they couldn't imagine the "depth of danger" (by which I assume he meant the pervasiveness of danger). It is a point I'll reluctantly concede. I say reluctantly because I don't want to scare you off. It would be a shame to miss this extravaganza, but I don't want to mislead you either. As far as I can tell, what's required of one is a persistent vigilance. It comes naturally.

When the poet W.H. Auden lived here he never left his apartment without a $5 bill in his pocket so if he were mugged, he would have something to offer by way of appeasement. We've taken a few precautions of our own. I never wear my good watch, and we do little walking and no subway riding at night—at night it's all cabs. I just read a piece about Manhattan by Jan Morris. She was talking about Central Park, which is both central to the city and central to the city's image as a dangerous place. "I have never been mugged in Central Park," she wrote, "never seen anyone else harmed either, but I have had my chill moments." This is what you can expect, dear—a chill moment here and there. But it's worth it.

Dear Bill,

We visited the Metropolitan Museum of Art this afternoon. You warned us not to wander aimlessly because there were 17 acres of it, so we went with a plan. Still, after three hours of masterpieces, I could feel my powers of appreciation starting to flag.

Cézanne, you know, has always been a favorite of mine. I thought I'd seen reproductions of almost everything he'd painted, but I found something new—for me anyway—*The Card Players*.

Also, in the sculpture gallery I couldn't help but notice *Ugolino and His Sons* by Carpeaux. While philosophically I'm not really sympathetic to this sort of theatricality, I have to admit that the larger-than-life drama of this complex piece stopped me in my tracks.

Dear Angie,

The other evening we were in a pizza joint on 35th Street. The owner, a large pot-bellied Italian, was sitting in the window, bellowing at the help. As he shouted orders, his barber lathered him up and commenced shaving. The barber was shaving him when we came in, and he was still shaving him when we left. The pizza, by the way, was great.

So far we haven't really noticed that rudeness for which New Yorkers are so famous. The least friendly people we've found are the bank tellers. If they're not sullen, they're surly. Usually they're surly. As we're always running out of money, we have more chances than we'd like to meet them.

The sheer amount of talent here is amazing. The jazz trio providing filler at Catch A Rising Star (a comedy club we went to last night) could have been a headline act anywhere else. Someone once said there were more good pianists playing in New York every evening than in the whole of Europe. It has to be true.

Dear Sue,

Do the wonders of New York outweigh the horrors? It depends on whether you're talking about visiting it or living in it. If you're talking about visiting it, the answer is yes—emphatically. If you are talking about living in it, the answer is no—with a few provisos. For living here to be anything other than exhausting you'd have to be young or rich. Because I am neither, I'll be seeing you Friday. You should, however, be warned: the me you'll be meeting won't be the one you said goodbye to. In New York, magic gets worked on even the most mundane. I've had my taste improved simply by coming here. I've picked up some flair, and I've upgraded my ingenuity.

Returning home from this is going to be a tricky business. I expect a cavalcade of anti-climaxes. One's perspective is inevitably changed, and the old hometown just can't be what she used to be. If I am lucky, that mechanism will come into play where over time one retains enough of their experience to be made wise but not so much as to be made unhappy.

MEETING THEM

So why are we doing this? We are doing this because she thinks it's a good idea—meeting my mother and father. She thinks on some level it will be fun. She wants to see where I come from so she can make an educated guess about where I am going and decide whether she wants to come along.

*

The subtle "it" of it all will begin right there at the front door. My mother will give her a short perfumed hug and my father one of his carefully calibrated handshakes—firm, but not too firm (manly, but not barbarous). My mother will smile and say something about it being nice to finally meet her, but she will say it with a tone—a tone that suggests some primitive grievance at the heart of her playfully implied complaint.

*

Dinner will be chicken something with rice. My mother—who has drawn her eyebrows on a little heavily—will begin the interrogation with a disarmingly tedious story about intrigue on the Board of the Homeowners Association. It will involve certain unscrupulous factions and their efforts to fund a new recreation center.

My father will say little because he doesn't want to be accused of being flirtatious. He will ask what her father does for a living. When he is told that her father is a dentist he will be pleased because if things go as it is theoretically possible they might and we are joined together in some sort of sanctioned union, there will be someone of means besides himself to assume the burden of my inevitable failure.

At some point my mother will ask her how we met—in part because she is interested but mostly because she wants to talk about how she and my father met. She never tires of the story (a missed digit in a telephone number), of feeling the cosmic quiver run up her back as she coolly contemplates the role sheer chance has played in the drama of their improbable introduction. If she hadn't done this and he hadn't done that—no them, no me, no us sitting here with chicken something and rice.

*

By the time we get to dessert the she who thought this was such a good idea will be uncomfortable—acutely conscious that things are not going well. She will feel she has talked too assertively—said unfortunate things about cats, about belief in an afterlife, about Republicans. She will begin to press. She will be effusive about the coffee and about me. Trying to flatter them as caregivers, she will ask what I was like as a child. They will struggle to find the appropriate euphemisms as they recall the poor grades, the substance abuse, the recalcitrance, the inadvertent poisoning of the Thompson girl. I was, they will say, something of a handful—an observation that will lead them to one of their favorite subjects: kids these days. Kids these days are, it seems—except for the hand/eye coordination they have developed playing video games—almost grotesquely inferior to the kids of other days.

*

Afterwards, as we drive home, she will be spookily quiet. I will feel the weight of her dejection fill the car. It will be a palpable thing, like humidity. They won't have been what she expected, but something else, something more depressing and consequently frightening. Their being this something else (whatever it is) will start her thinking and worrying and asking questions—questions that only have questions for answers, questions about me, questions about us, about the future. She will turn the radio on. I will remember the song that is playing forever as our song, the one we listened to that rainy night when the end of something promising began and the middle of it simply was no more.

MADDIE'S MANTRAS

I'm pudding for breakfast. I'm a breath mint at the garlic festival of your day. I'm a ten-dollar bill in the wallet of love. I'm the palm of reason on Malarkey Island. I'm a rare moogoo in a world of gai pan. I'm a glittering scrunchie in the hairdo of hatred. I'm that little plastic thingamajig on the end that keeps the shoelace of romance from fraying. I'm a slice of cheese on the boring burger of being. I put the bop in the bop-she bop-she bop. I'm a little can of Sterno in the igloo of a cold man's heart. I'm a polished bone in the primitive nose of negativism. I'm the meringue on the lemon pie of life. I'm the tuxedo on the penguin of pleasure. I'm the "Color" in Colorado and the "Ten" in Tennessee. (Never mind about Virginia.) I'm the dazzling doodad that hangs from the rearview mirror of history. I'm the cashmere collar on a barbed-wire sweater. I'm loose change under the sofa cushions of poverty. I'm the gooey center of redemption in a bonbon for Beelzebub. I'm a feather in the cap of freedom. I'm chili powder on the cornflakes of conformity. I'm a silver bullet in the bandoleer of desperate appeals. I'm the fuzz on the tennis ball of happiness. I'm a flowerbed in the quagmire of the quotidian. I'm that extra gallon when the gas gauge reads "empty." I'm a room-service vodka at The Heartbreak Hotel. I'm the brassy shine on the tuba of tomorrow. I'm a lava lamp in the mineshaft of mediocrity. I'm a soft spot on the armadillo of intolerance. I'm a jagged shard of truth caught in the throat of blatant dissimulation. I'm super.

WILL THERE BE DUCKS?

What do you think when you first see him? Not much. You think we must be moving on to someone else, someone you could recognize ten minutes from now if you had to, someone with a little more character in his face, someone with some lines here and there, someone with an unusual nose or one of those cleft chins. But no, this is him. Steven. Steven Skidmore. Mr. Easy-Not-To-Notice, Mr. Likes-His-Carbohydrates, Mr. Nothing Special. Look at that sad tie. Is this Everyman? Is that what I'm up to here? What if I say he was born in Nebraska. Do I need to say anything else? Do I need to say he's white? Do I need to say he is 35 years old? Do I need to say he believes in beef, baseball, and straight talking—that he is, on some level, embarrassed to be feeling rarified, unmanly things?

What does the bar look like? It looks like the Kingston before they remodeled. Lots of dark wood and scuffed vinyl. A warm, yeasty-smelling place—a place where lots of things are sticky that shouldn't be.

He's thinking about what—all the money he owes, how he hates his job, how he wishes Randall, the guy in the cubicle next to him, would say something interesting for just once in his life?

*

When he leaves the bar is he drunk? A little, maybe. Certain things come closer than usual to making sense, and he's more likely than he might otherwise have been to be precise in the sentences he imagines. So how does he get hit in the face? Does he run into someone in the parking lot—a feral, predatory youth, the sort we like to hold up as an example to others of just what can happen when mothers are drug-addicted or teachers insufficiently nurturing—someone pierced, and tattooed, a player of hacky sack, a haver of bad attitudes? No. He clips a light pole as he is driving out of the parking lot.

A light pole?

He's distracted. Someone he has seen in the bar has reminded him vaguely of Pamela Engebretson, a girl he knew in high school. He is mesmerized for a moment by the vividness of what he can remember—the shade of her tan, the texture of her favorite sweater, the beadiness of her optometrist father's eyes. He is trying to say her name out loud when he turns a little too sharply and catches the pole with twenty-five pounds of classic American-made front bumper, snapping it at the base. The lantern part of the light—a thing roughly the size and shape of a rural mailbox—comes smashing through the windshield of his sad little rattletrap. It happens quickly and is a complete surprise to everyone.

*

Steven drives off.

Can we hear what's playing on his radio as we watch the glow of his taillights recede into the distance? Maybe. It's that song by whatshisname, isn't it? The one Nick has identified as "spine tingling"—capable of making a person question his unquestioning faith in the literal.

Is this sudden confrontation with fortuity an intimation of things to come? Is it the spark that starts some sort of psychic and/or thematic fire? Is it the sort of thing a reader's guide might refer to: "In the opening of the story, Steven Skidmore, the main character, is hit in the face by a falling lamp. What is the significance of this 'accident'?"

*

Does Steven have anyone waiting for him at home— anyone who could or would help him pick the glass out of his face? No. Not since "she" (whose name we do not mention) moved out.

So?

So he drives his lonesome, battered, bloodied self to the nearest hospital emergency room where he is treated expeditiously and released.

*

How do Kathy and Christine act when Steven walks into the office the next morning? Just as you would imagine.

Steven tries to pass off his swollen, stitched-up hideousness as nothing really worth talking about, but Kathy, who has an appetite for life and can't help herself, wants a full plate of details so he invents an 80-year-old woman, an intersection, and a 1996 pearl-white Cadillac Seville with automatic transmission and leather seats.

My Desk and I

Do Kathy and Christine have auto accident stories of their own to tell? Of course.

Kathy's involves a rear-end collision in which her little dog, a shiatsu named Suzie, is thrown into the dashboard and knocked out. (When it awakens it has a completely different personality.)

And Christine's? Christine's involves the death of a child—a cousin's son. He was seven. What is Steven thinking as he listens to her? Does he recall some tragic incident in his own life—a younger brother drowned in the backyard pool, a pretty neighbor girl inadvertently poisoned? Is that what this is about—a buried and deforming pain? Is he wearing the right facial expression for someone listening to such a story? What should he say? How can people tell you something like this? What do they want? Can it be provided? How will he fail them?

*

What about the backstory? Who is Everyman? Where did he go to school? What sort of jobs did he have before he ended up with this one? He used to be one way, now he's another. Does he know why?

*

Next morning. The alarm clock goes off. Is he a heavy sleeper or an insomniac?

Trying to shave around all of his cuts and stitches is a challenge. With all that swelling and his nose still pointing off in the wrong direction, he can barely recognize himself—he looks like some sort of laboratory experiment gone wrong. As he stares at the mess in front of him he remembers his first fistfight. It was with a boy named Alan Peacock. What was it about? He has no idea. He does, however, remember wishing it had been with someone else, someone more popular, someone more coordinated, someone whose defeat would have bequeathed him greater honor.

What's sitting there on the counter for us to see? A ceramic cup, a soap dispenser, a radio. He turns on NPR and listens to a story about what? About a cinnamon bun that looks like Mother Teresa. It's been stolen from a coffeehouse in Nashville. Steven remembers Nashville. He drove through it once when he was five. He was in a station wagon with his mother. She was smoking and talking non-stop about the miraculous new life they were going to have in Seattle.

What was he thinking about as he watched the highway flying by? He was thinking about the life he was leaving behind, a life where he and his friends used to chase each other for no reason, where they used to throw oranges at the ghosts in his grandmother's garage. And? And he was wondering about the new life—the one he was heading toward. Was there going to be anything to do in it, anyone to do it with? Would it be a life of cereal that was good for him, a life spent in the kitchen listening to his mother cry in front of the stove? Would there be ducks where they are going? Would there be a boat?

*

Steven is sitting at his desk. He looks overwhelmed by the insignificant day-in day-out sameness of his job. He stares silently into space as he taps a mock SOS on the keyboard of his computer. Is this a story about the mysterious workings of the human heart, about the disastrous consequences of a failure to ignore the logical conclusions that have been made inevitable by the spirit of the age?

*

At home we watch him make what sort of dinner for himself? Is it some sad little frozen thing like a potpie or an elaborate, gourmetish production that involves lots of fancy preparation and expertise? What about coriander and cumin? It would be nice, wouldn't it, to have their scents seep into a paragraph.

Later he sits down in front of the television. He has a beer. What is he watching? Should it be something that has some sort of oblique connection to the theme of the story or something that suggests the previously unsuggested?

More deep, quiet regret. Is he a man pursued by a knowledge of his limitations? Look at the way he sits: it's the classic posture of defeat. What's he thinking? Is it about Laura who he lived with for six months? Laura who started working on a committee to save Mill Pond, who started coming home late. Laura who for some reason didn't seem excited about him any more, who stopped answering his questions, who started getting telephone calls that were difficult to explain. Laura who moves out and takes his most flattering estimation of himself with her.

Is this story about loneliness? What about fate? Identity? Being enlightened? What about pitiless truth-telling, a decent man's passage, the mystery of things as they should be? What about the case for counting cats in Zanzibar?

*

The lantern—a thing roughly the size and shape of a rural mailbox—has smashed through his windshield. He has driven off. What if he just stays on the road? What if he drives and drives until there is only blackness, until he runs out of gas? What if he sits in his car at the side of the road until someone passing stops to ask if he is ok? If he doesn't answer what would happen? Who would be called? Would he be lifted out of the front seat by large men? Would he be placed on a stretcher? Where would he be taken?

*

Morning. Steven is in a coffee shop about a block from his office. He is sitting alone with a cup of espresso, not noticing anything around him, reading a piece of newspaper he has taken from the empty table next to him. What is the story? Is it about the Department of Human Services budget, the new Opera Center, the kidnapped coed?

*

He runs into Gary Doyle at the elevator. Does he know him very well? No. Gary works in credit.
What floor?
Six, please.
Apropos of nothing, Gary brings up the subject of

what? His son. Apparently he has just won a prize at his school's science fair. His project involved measuring the amount of bacteria to be found in various samples of ice.

*

And what about Amanda in order production? Does he have a little thing for her? She's a doctor's daughter. She went to an expensive school and is now living with an overweight man who refinishes wood floors for a living. How does she feel about Steven? She seems to like him, but she seems to like everybody. Is this what the story is about—Steven's unrequited feelings for Amanda? A little late to introduce her isn't it? How big are her eyes? What color is her hair? What does he want to say to her? He wants to say something that cuts through the trivial, something that takes a chip out of the foundation of a significant proposition—but in a funny way. He wants to say something that will make her think and laugh. Something that will make her respect him. He wants to say something that could make a difference were the situation somehow other than what it was.

*

Maybe he should go for a walk at lunch. It would be good to get him outside where the wonders of nature could be anthropomorphized and the reader alerted to the author's ungrudging reverence for a certain type of award-winning prosody. The leaves on the trees could be curling at the corners like coy but villainous smiles. The clouds could glide across the distant horizon like so many gossamer galleons. Maybe this would be the place to put the panhandler—the one with the fishing pole. Steven stops and gives him something. How much? Not much. He saves his silver for later. (Each afternoon at 2:15 p.m. he wanders down to the lunchroom where he gets himself a carton of milk and a bag of chocolate chip cookies.)

*

Steven walks into Tim Cumming's office to complain about yet another pointless report he has been asked to put together by someone I will probably call Davidson. Why is he really here? He's really here because certain pressures seem to be building. His face hurts. His landlady hates him. He's being devoured at night by his very own Steven-ness. Things seem to be going places even though he doesn't want them to, and he thinks Tim, being the sort of person he is—an obviously-troubled-but-still-together sort—might be able to help. And is he? Not really.

Steven tries to steer the conversation toward what are to him the pertinent issues but is unsuccessful as Tim is preoccupied with a jammed stapler and a detailed account of his latest recurring nightmare.

*

Saturday. He has gone to an early movie and is now following a girl he noticed there as she walks off down the street. It is some sort of game he has decided to play with himself—a test. A test of what? Does he know? Does the reader know?

My Desk and I

What do you think when you first see her? You think she must be the one. Why even look anywhere else? This is her: Miss Stands-Out-In-A-Crowd, Miss Watches-Her-Weight, Miss Cleaner-Than-Clean. What if I said she was born in California? Do I need to say anything else? Do I need to say she is blonde? Do I need to say she is 22? Do I need to say the air around her is different than the air around everyone else?

Steven follows her into a card shop. She is buying what—a birthday card for her mother. Pretending to be looking at cards himself, he gets close enough to read the one she is holding: "No matter where life may lead me, I'll always be thankful for who you are." Really? No. This girl's mother has told her terrible things about her father, things a truly special mother would never tell a daughter. She has destroyed part of the girl's memory of him because he never made her as happy as she felt she deserved to be.

What about Steven's mother? Was he thankful for who she was? No. An alcoholic suicide, he had to stop feeling much about her one way or the other a long time ago.

In getting close enough to read the card Steven has made the girl nervous and uneasy. His battered face suggests what to her? Cravenness? Criminality? She knows he has followed her. Does she say anything to him? Maybe she tries to inch away. Maybe she goes to the woman behind the cash register and asks for help. Is a security person called? Is that what this story is about—Steven devolving before our eyes into something creepy?

Does he do something theatrical here—something denouement-like? Does he try to kiss the girl and get wrestled to the ground and handcuffed? Does this become a story about doing hard time, about drooling cellmates with hairy backs and rustic diction? Or does he do something smaller, something into which just about anything can be read? Maybe he just walks off into the sunset? Can we hear what he is whistling? It's that song by whatshisname, isn't it? The one Nick has identified as "spine tingling"—capable of making a person question his unquestioning faith in the literal. What about something midway between big and little? Maybe he introduces himself to the girl and apologizes just before the guard arrives. He tells her that she reminds him of someone. He tells her about the parking lot, about getting hit in the face, about the lantern—a thing roughly the size and shape of a rural mailbox. They go for a cup of coffee. There is some sort of subtle connection being made that suggests this could be the beginning of something. What? Does he know? Does the reader know? What about Amanda? Will there be ducks where they are going? Will there be a boat?

HELLO, HELLO, HELLO

Hello, hello, hello—it's me. I don't know why I'm writing to you. What's the point? Maybe I think you'll write back and we'll become great friends and when you're in Portland next—to do a reading before a frightening throng of admirers—you'll call me up and we'll go get pizza at this special place I go to all the time over on Twenty-Third. You'll tell me stories about the comic ordeal of the book tour, and I'll tell you stories about the comic ordeal of growing up in Santa Clara—about a swimming pool and making a primitive sort of aqua-lung out of an old canister vacuum cleaner and almost electrocuting myself. I'll pick up the tab for the pizza (which will be a medium pepperoni supreme, by the way), and you'll reach out with your pointer finger—like Michelangelo's God—and pass the spark of life to me.

Why am I writing to you? I don't know. In part I guess it's because I just finished your new book last night, and as I was sitting there in my lucky chair—full of alcohol and admiration (for the thing as a whole, but especially for stories one, four, eight, and eleven)—I remembered you saying somewhere in an interview that you wanted to write something as valuable as the Lorrie Moore story, "People Like That Are the Only People Here." I was excited when I read that because I am a deeply dyed-in-the-wool Lorrie Moore fan myself. I know and admire and was completely overwhelmed by that story too. I remember feeling some sort of extra connection to you, some sort of impulse to wave hello, hello, hello like people in the same make of car sometimes do when they are passing on the highway. For some reason I wanted to tell you that we shared a love for this story (and for Lorrie Moore herself) and to respond to the request for affirmation I felt was implied in your stated wish by saying, in my opinion, you had written something as valuable: your third novel.

Why am I writing to you? I don't know. In part it's because I know how hard it is to do what you're trying to do, and I want to encourage you to continue to try to do it. I want to tell you that you have touched someone in the way you have wanted to in the hope that knowing of this success will, in some small way, make some of the sacrifices you are making seem worth it. And, you know, blah, blah, blah, blah, blah....

I read—in the strange letter you wrote and published about feeding squirrels in your backyard—that as a famous writer who has had one of his books made into a movie, you get lots and lots of writer-related mail. People send you all sorts of things, including copies of their stories. Did you ever do something like that when you were getting started—send a copy of one of your stories to someone like you? It never occurred to me to do something like that, but maybe it should have. I really don't have any idea of how the literary world works. I'd send you a copy of the story I'm working on now, but it isn't finished. That's probably another reason I'm writing to you—so I don't have to be working on this story, which I have come not to like very much. It's about an institutionalized man who is waiting for a visit from a woman

he sees regularly, a woman with whom he has had a relationship but now he doesn't entirely recognize, and, in
fact, suspects of being an undercover agent working for
his doctor. As he's waiting, he's making a list in his head
of all the things he is not going to talk about, things that
could end up in his file, things like his stealing a trombone from the music room or his fantasies of lifting his
past girlfriends up over his head one at a time. Things
like the night before when he had that feeling again—the
one he gets all the time.

In some ways it would make perfect sense to send
this to you because I know you've been institutionalized
and I bet you would have some valuable things to say—
as pertains to scenes and settings and procedures and
such—but I can't get past the bumptiousness of the idea
that a writer who writes like you write, who is famous
and has had one of his novels made into a movie, would
have nothing better to do with two, three, maybe even
four hours of his night than to read and make notes on
some complete stranger's uninspired, half-finished short
story about the sad intractability of fear.

As I'm writing now I am a little uncertain about your
domestic situation, and I'm assuming this is something
you have intended. I don't know where I got the idea you
were married, but as I remember it there was a small
half-sentence mention somewhere. When I read this I was
surprised because I'd never heard any kind of mention of
it before.

I'm also a little confused about where you live. In one
article someone is calling you at your apartment in Brooklyn, and then the next thing I know—in the aforemen-
tioned letter about squirrel watching—you live in some

small, rural, upstate town that has a two-lady post office and no garbage pick-up so you have to take your trash down to the dump yourself. In this rural home you are apparently living near your father (who must be pretty old now and who used to be some sort of highly successful business person) who sometimes comes to visit and mistakes one of the sorts of squirrels that come to your feeders for another. I thought you were estranged? Maybe you were during your long journey through the nightmare of alcohol and drugs and psychiatric hospitals, and now that you are clean and sober and pray and have had one of your novels made into a movie, you are reunited?

My own domestic situation—or as much as I'm willing to offer up as penitence for my presumption—is as follows:

I'm divorced. I live alone in a small, slightly dilapidated, L-shaped apartment, and this past weekend I went to the beach. I had a wonderful time. I stayed at the place I always try to stay, had seafood stew, and visited a friend named Harry Bennett, an eighty-year old expressionist painter who likes to wear his work shirts tucked in. When I came home three days later—all mellow from the sound of the surf and my visit with the life-affirming Harry—I found my refrigerator had died. Everything in it was ruined, including a dozen of the frozen dinners I am reluctant to admit to anyone that I eat. It (the refrigerator) was just standing there stinking in a congealed pool of caramel-colored gunk. I had to hold my nose and empty it out. I had to have the maintenance men come in and wheel it away. As they did, they took huge chunks of wood out of three different door jambs.

As for my father, he was decapitated in an automobile accident in 1985.

When that reporter in Philadelphia asked if you enjoyed reading tours, you said no, you didn't enjoy the tours but you enjoyed meeting readers. You said you were willing to go through the unpleasantness of the tour to meet people who found something important in what you do. Well hello, hello, hello—I'm sparing you the jet lag, the hotel food, the strained chit-chat with the media escort—you are meeting one of those people right now on this page, one of those people who finds something important in what you do.

And hello again, this goes right to the heart of the trouble I'm having writing this. If I were about to have my (as yet unwritten) novel published, I would be doing everything I could—via the usual plenipotentiaries: agents, editors, lawyers, etc.—to avoid a tour. I wouldn't really have any interest in meeting anyone who was to me what I am to you—that is, someone who found something important in what I did. While I can be flattered to some degree, I'm afraid I'm not the sort of person who could be encouraged to continue to do what I was doing by a letter from someone like me. On the subject of writing, I'm not really interested in anything less than the best expert opinion.

As there is basically no letter that could encourage me, I'm having trouble imagining what sort of letter to write to someone who some sort of letter might. In your case I don't think it should be some gushing thing because I can't say I have any sense that you are the sort of person who could be prompted by that. I don't know what such a letter should be—other than sincere, and honest, and maybe intelligent. Can I write such a letter? Well, that's another question.

Why am I writing to you? I just don't know. If you have any ideas, maybe you could drop me a line. One of the things I have always liked about your stuff is its directness, its freedom from the usual sort of knee-jerk charitability one finds in so much enlightened work. My guess is you could be illuminating—though I'm sure I wouldn't be able to agree with your pitiless conclusions.

Anyway, if you are here, thank you for taking the time to have come this far. I hope you don't feel like you've completely wasted it; I know it's valuable. I would hate to think I've slowed down the production of your wonderful sentences, so I'm not going to. I'm going to imagine the time you spent reading this is time you would otherwise have spent cleaning up some part of your apartment (or house?) in an effort to make it appear (to the company coming) that you were a tidier or neater person than you actually are. I'm going to imagine you would have been doing something like vacuuming a hallway or picking up some clothes that were left lying around someplace they shouldn't have been.

Yours appreciatively—me.

LINE DRIVE

Baseball was the second or transitional stage of what David thinks of as his three-staged adolescence. (First there was his interest in science—chemistry and astronomy mostly, stories in themselves; then his interest in sports; then, of course, his interest in women.) He was an average hitter for his age and size and an average fielder, but when it came to pitching, he was lucky enough to be something very close to special. He had a fastball that was way ahead of its time. He came to it by accident. He had apparently inherited a talent in this direction, which he inadvertently developed throwing grapefruit at the neighbors.

When David was eight, he moved into a new development of ranch-style homes on what was then the outskirts of Phoenix, Arizona. Most of the area had been citrus groves at one time. David grew up playing with the neighbor kids in the orchards that remained. Playing meant a lot of things, but invariably it meant at some point throwing grapefruit at one another. The better you were at this—the more accurate you were, the farther you could throw—the better your chances of fending off attack. A decent grapefruit weighs about a pound and a half. David developed his arm strength by throwing them a good forty or fifty yards, usually at a fleeing Mark Barnes. Throwing a baseball, which was about 5 ounces, at a stationary target a mere forty-four feet away—that was nothing.

*

David has a team photo that he cannot find, but he knows is around here somewhere. It is black and white, but he can remember quite clearly the unlovely, old-dollar-bill-green of their uniforms. In the minor leagues, these uniforms consisted of t-shirts and caps. In the majors—to which everyone aspired for sartorial reasons, if no other—you got pants and socks and, in fact, were rigged up to look like a sort of miniature pro. The team was called the Solons—a name David and the others hated. It meant nothing to them. It didn't resonate with any of the testosterone-infused deno- or connotations they would have preferred, but apparently it meant something to the small sporting-goods store that modestly sponsored them because it was insisted on in the face of their strenuous objections.

In the photo the kids were arranged in three rows. Gangly, buck-toothed, big-eared, they were ten and eleven-year-olds caught midway through puberty. In most cases they would never look goofier.

David was in the front row on the left end, kneeling with his perfectly beat-up mitt. His cap is on straight, its bill unique. It is not like the bill of any other cap. It is squared off, creased on each side with an emphatic precision that hints at a blossoming predisposition.

David didn't know anything about pitching, but he wasn't expected to. His hero was Whitey Ford—mostly because he was a New York Yankee. (If David had known anything about pitching, his hero would have been Sandy Koufax.) David had only one pitch: a fastball that he threw as hard as he could right down the middle. He never threw anything clever—no curves, no corners, no splitter. He didn't go high or low, inside or out. Just as fast and right down the middle as he could.

David was in the minor leagues for two years, and for those two years he was considered one of the top two pitchers. The other top pitcher was a guy named Hogan, who was considerably larger than David. Although he never said anything about it to anyone, he always suspected Hogan had gotten into their particular division on some sort of technicality.

David was proud of his reputation, puffed up about it in the way only a ten-year-old can be puffed up—but he didn't have then, and he doesn't have now, any sense of that pride extending very far afield. If there were certain "global" effects, they were definitely with a little "g." David became insufferable only on game day and only within a quarter-mile radius of the diamond. Knowing who he was as a pitcher had very little to do with knowing who he was as a son or a brother or an anything else for that matter.

*

It is generally understood that as self-esteem is nurtured by success, it can be damaged by failure. If Little League Baseball proved to be a source of some of David's more significant moments of triumph, it was also the source of some of his most significant moments of defeat. One in particular stands out. It was near the end of his last season. He was pitching in a big game, an early-round playoff, and there was a crowd considerably larger than he was used to. There were probably a couple hundred people there, but it seemed like thousands to him. When he was on the mound he was keenly aware of people milling on the periphery of his vision, a sort of foaming along the sidelines. It was hot and there was lots of noise, the usual hey-batter, hey-batter, hey-batter chatter from the infield together with all sorts of exhortations from the family-filled bleachers.

It was about midpoint in the game, and David was cruising. He was in that eerie, slightly mystical psychic place—jockdom's state of grace—that would later come to be known in sportsbabble as "the zone." He started the inning with a quick strikeout. He had a small lead so he had no inhibitions. He can't say that his first and most furious pitch to the next batter was a strike, but he thinks it was likely because of what he can remember clearly about the second pitch, the one the guy hit. David was feeling, for perhaps a nanosecond, that it was beautiful, a perfect strike, and that he was about to be sitting pretty, way ahead in the count. That nanosecond's elation was ruined by the crack of the bat. David's perfect pitch—hard, right down the middle—was lined perfectly right back at him. He was not an equipment-wearing pitcher, and the line drive hit him where, as a young male, he least wanted to be hit. In front of all those people he was dropped like a rock. He laid curled up fetally on the mound trying to keep the moaning and crying to a minimum.

David was carried off the field. If this public injury was not humiliating enough, there was the semi-public first aid. He was carried to a nearby snack stand (manned by girls—who, as he remembers, were definitely in the cute category) where he had his pants packed with snowcones.

David has read the current literature on trauma. He understands the trend in some notorious places is to believe this sort of experience has physiological consequences—the idea being that certain chemical responses to stimuli beget certain other chemical responses which in turn beget certain other chemical responses which in turn beget actual anatomical changes in the brain—changes in such things as neurotransmitter pathways that, depending on the nature and severity of the experience, can subtly or not-so-subtly change the way you think and feel forever.

As a young repressor David didn't talk about this catastrophic event—he just moved on. If the reported physiological effects on the brain were true, however, he couldn't help but wonder about the enduring consequences. He did not attribute any of the grosser malformations of his character to the event, but he did wonder if there was not some seemingly insignificant something somewhere that he felt just a little bit different about as a result. He wondered if this something had played an unanticipatedly significant part in his subsequent thought processes. Who knows in the chaos of succeeding cognitive life—the cascading multiplicity of connections and disconnections—but that getting hit in the balls twenty years ago had something to do with the way he felt today about speed-skating, the Department of Motor Vehicles, or Shakespeare.

David doesn't want to suggest his baseball experience was a wash—he got much more out of it than he lost. But still, all these years later, when recollecting—as for this story, for example—the sensation of that success (which supposedly paved the way to his becoming a productive member of society) is vague whereas that line drive (which might have influenced his position on capital punishment or federal funding for the arts) is vivid. In fact, it still has the power to double him up.

TOP DRAWER

You know better, but what difference does it make. Knowing better has never stopped you before. It isn't something you are particularly proud of, this character deficiency, this moral imperfection, but it's something you can live with—quite easily as a matter of fact.

As it so happens, it is August and you are staying at the beach with your parents and the Caldwells. The Caldwells, for reasons not entirely clear to you, seem genuinely fond of your mother and father. They have, in a sense, adopted them. No one you know will call the Caldwells "rich" because that would be gauche, but they are—"rich." They have a huge house in the city and this more-than-ample one here. The house in the city has pillars out front and is at the end of a long, curved drive that is lined with small, symmetrical hedges linked like so many leafy sausages. This one, the beach house, is covered with white clapboards. It is cornily Cape Coddish. Each summer the Caldwells invite your parents to visit; each summer your parents invite you. The Caldwells are older, somewhere in their sixties; their children are long gone. You—you are too young to have flown. Here at the beach it is your lot in life to be superfluous—and superfluous you are, with a vengeance.

Right now Max and Judith have taken your parents out to feed the seagulls leftover veal Viennese. You have the house to yourself, and, conscienceless soul that you are, you have wandered into the master bedroom. You have not been able to resist going through the top drawer of the Caldwells' dresser. Top drawers are catnip to you. You know from your own top drawer and the top drawers of those closest to you that it is in these simple vaults that the secrets of personality reside.

The Caldwells' dresser is a large one. It is dark and elaborately carved. On top of it sits a long beveled mirror in which you watch yourself trespass. You pull the drawer open. It is heavy, but it glides out easily. You know this is the sign of a good dresser, a quality dresser—a truly expensive dresser. You compare the action of this top drawer to the actions of all the top drawers you have known before. This is the best.

The first thing you find are eyeglasses. There are at least two dozen pair. It occurs to you that the Caldwells must inhabit a special place in their optometrist's heart. You try on several pair of Caldwells' glasses. Each has a different correction; each transforms you immediately, makes you look older, more serious, more intelligent—too intelligent to be doing what you are doing. You try on several pair of Mrs. Caldwell's glasses. They too are different prescriptions. Mrs. Caldwell's taste runs to the ornate and outlandishly feminine. They make you look ridiculous. You get a headache. It is a slightly frightening, slightly comic thing to contemplate—these people's ever-changing view of the world.

Under a lacy scarf you find a large pair of silver nail clippers. You have never seen a pair of clippers this large before. Must be the sea air. You find keys—keys of every sort: office keys, house keys, car keys, key keys. It is, you notice, a rule of thumb: the better off someone is, the more keys they have. They are awarded—like medals.

You find cufflinks shaped like golf clubs, aqua-colored jars of facial goop, old airline tickets, a half-empty bottle of thick, chalk-tasting antacid. In one corner you find a cigarette lighter that doesn't work; in another, a small brown vial of pills with the directions "Take as needed." You find a set of tortoise-shell hairbrushes and a pouch of pliable white collar-stays. You find a gold heart, a bag of cotton balls, a shoehorn, a packet of bone buttons, and a pamphlet titled "Life as a Non-Smoker."

What you don't find is what you most avidly seek—something sexual.

Your interest, in truth, is shamefully earthbound—it is, in a word, prurient. What was a top drawer without something sexual in it? You think of your own top drawer and the pictures you have torn from magazines and hidden in the bottom of the plastic case your Timex came in. You think of the prophylactics you have found, the tubes of mysterious ointment. You will never forget the Larkin's top drawer where, in all its splendor, sat Mrs. Larkin's diaphragm—a thing whose implications were simply too hormonally huge for you to handle. These were top drawers worthy of the name.

When everyone gets back from the beach they call for you. You present yourself as quickly and as innocently as you can. Mrs. Caldwell is holding a pair of high heels in one hand and a clean china platter in the other. Apparently the gulls have been ravenous. ". . . . and she never knew what hit her," you hear Mr. Caldwell say, finishing what is obviously a joke. Everyone laughs in that winking, annoyingly naughty, adult way. Before you know it, you have asked Mr. Caldwell how old he is—exactly. Your parents are mortified. Mr. Caldwell struggles to seem good-natured. He runs a hand through his gray hair and answers you with a cliché: "Don't let the snow on the roof fool you, Paul. There's still a fire in the furnace."

You know better, but what difference does it make.

RICHARD INTRODUCES HIMSELF

Thank you. I was going to say it was nice to be here, but of course you know it isn't. Not really. I mean its better to be here than nowhere, but...well, you know what I'm getting at. I can tell by all that bobble-doll headshaking.

I guess I should start with my name—it's Richard. I was born in Baltimore, Maryland, but I don't really make a big deal out of it. As I understand it, there are people who do. I can't imagine why. Maybe we could discuss that later.

So what first...my unremarkable childhood I suppose. It was pretty much normal as far as I can tell. I grew up wearing ugly T-shirts and loving all the stuff I was supposed to—ice cream, playing outside, television. I got my first spanking at the age of five (for punching my sister in the stomach) and my first dog at the age of eight. His name was Boots. He was run over by a neighbor with a low IQ.

At ten I wanted to be a scientist. I was particularly interested in rockets. I built them from kits. My father would take me out Saturday mornings to a nearby park and let me shoot them off. These rockets were powered by small gunpowder-filled engines that looked like rolls of quarters. At the top of each engine was a small reverse-blast section. Once the fuel was burned up in the ascent, this back-blast would blow the nosecone off the rocket allowing a small, colorful parachute to deploy.

One afternoon when I was home alone, I decided to launch one of these rockets from my backyard. It went astray. It lost a tailfin at blastoff and corkscrewed across the street. It flew into the Osborne's house and stuck in the livingroom ceiling. When the back-blast went off it started a fire in the attic.

In high school I took an interest in acting. Because I had a good memory and a natural scowl, I was given the part of Iago in a thoroughly lackluster production of *Othello*. At our final dress rehearsal I had an accident. I was struggling with a speech in Act 2 when I stepped off the stage and fell into the orchestra pit. I landed on my head, getting a concussion, a gash above my eye, and the first of the three rides I have had in ambulances. There was talk of the school having been negligent. A settlement was made.

I had my first coital experience at the age of sixteen— though I frequently lie about this and claim to have had it at the age of twelve. The object of my affection was a shiny blond girl named Shelly. We were together for almost two years.

In college I fell under the influence of a professor by the name of Maywood and became a Platonist. I rented a small studio apartment, ate nothing but raisins and yogurt, and sought to live a life devoted to the contemplation of eternal truths. I was well on the way to achieving self-mastery when I met Pamela Hershey. She popped up out of the English Department in a tight yellow sweater and introduced into my life some eloquent arguments for the primacy of passion. We moved into a little cottage that was paneled with knotty pine. Six months later she found someone with a more arbitrary sense of fun.

My Desk and I

When I graduated I took a job as a statistical analyst for a company that sold burglar alarms. I tracked national crime rates and reported what I found to our sales and marketing departments. I did this for almost three years. I quit when I realized my daily immersion in this pond of toxic numbers had transformed me from a relatively calm and confident individual into a highly agitated and fearful one. I developed a drinking problem and went to Arizona for eight weeks to recover.

When I returned I was a new man. I was dried out and in touch with my transcendent side. I took a job with a company that published investment newsletters. I was with them for almost a year, but left when a disagreement about just what did and did not constitute ethical business practices got out of hand and I was put in the position of having to say some things that nobody really wanted to hear.

I have been in my new position at Fidelity Insurance for almost a month now and am enjoying it very much. Each morning at 9:45 a.m. I wander down to the second floor lunchroom where I get myself a piece of gooey apple strudel. By an expensive and time-consuming process of elimination, I have determined this strudel to be the most consistently palatable thing to be found in the Fidelity vending machines. Sealed in cellophane, it's folded over like a wallet and decorated with gravelly grains of sugar. I recommend it to anyone who might be interested.

SOME THINGS HE'S THROWN AWAY THIS YEAR

1
_____

From a discarded short story titled "My Guy":

My guy is my guy by default. (My real guy decided not to run at the last minute because a set of exploratory polls suggested—for a second time—that he was still not perceived as inherently likable enough to be viable.) I sort of gravitated to this guy—let's call him X—with a bunch of other back-of-the-bus types because he was a pro and he was in it. One of the things he has made clear he wants from us (almost more than any other thing) is an effort vis-a-vis the media because that's the kind of guy he is—a cautious, cultivate-the-media, don't-upset-anybody-if-you-don't-have-to kind of guy. The kind of guy who on one level frustrates me, but on another level encourages me to subordinate that frustration.

2
_____

From a discarded poem titled "Just Me":

Pay no attention,
it's just me

and my mood disorder.
Just me with my brooding frown,
my lethargy,
my cautious contempt.
Just me—
a pill away from perfect.
Just me
tipped over
by the quiet despair.
Just me
held down
by the unfriendly vision
of a brief and arbitrary finitude—
by the flattering,
French inclination
to believe in the authenticity
of a nihilistic anguish.

3

From a discarded essay titled "Infinity and Me":

There is probably an ideal age to begin contemplating something like "infinity," but I have no idea what it is. I'm pretty sure it isn't eight—at least it wasn't for me. As a complex piece of inspired imagining it wasn't, of course, something I just came up with. It was handed to me by a gaga grandpa—a biology professor who at one point in his life looked very much like the English philosopher Bertrand Russell (same hair, same rodential muzzle, same beaky nose). He was always giving me stuff he shouldn't—like a pocket knife, sips from his martini, a nightmare-inducing story about flesh-eating bacteria.

4

From a discarded poem titled "No Memos Today":

There are no memos today,
no nice neat blocks
of businessy bullshit
to make the world go round.
No memos
because he does not feel
suitably sonorous or incantory.
Instead he feels small
and stupid—
capable only of making telephone calls
to people who are easy.

5

From a discarded short story titled "Midnight":

When I look back on it from the relative comfort of the here and now it seems disorientingly strange. It's not the sort of thing I would expect someone like me to get caught up in. If someone like me were to get caught up in something, I would expect it to be something entirely different. If someone like me were to get caught up in something like this there would have to be an explanation. It would have to have something to do with brain chemistry and what happens to a person when they are deprived of sleep.

6

From a discarded (unfinished) novel titled "The 34-Pound Dog":

Let's skip the lobby where I run into a couple of the colorful characters who reside here and follow me up in the elevator to 901 where I set my bag of frozen dinners down in the kitchen and then let my dog Toby out of a padlocked bathroom.

Toby is a mix—of exactly what, no one knows for sure, but judging from the ad hoc look of him, it seems likely he is, in significant proportions, beagle, boxer, and something probably poodle-like. The mix is important because the whole that is the sum of its parts can't weigh more than 35 pounds or I am in violation of my lease agreement and consequently subject to eviction. This is just what Mrs. Dorton, the evil manageress, wants.

7

From a discarded essay titled "Dollars and Dollops":

I've come close to buying one of Brian's pictures three times: twice from the gallery that represents him and once from a grizzled old coot of a collector who got himself in over his head with his obsessive art purchases and was selling off some things in an effort to save his house. Each time I hesitated. Each time I walked away. Each time I wondered why.

8

From a discarded poem titled "A Few Things":

There are a few
things every day
that make it one way
and not another:
The blue umbrella
my neighbor puts out on his patio
(although everyone has asked him nicely not to)
that suggests a blindness to beauty,
an indifference to suffering,
a disdain for the rule of law.
The feel of something
on the side of my neck
that wasn't there before
that suggests waiting rooms,
cold stethoscopes, paper gowns,
and oblivion.

9

From a discarded short story titled "Penmanship":

Arthur's script has never been very good. It lacks everything good script should have: balance, beauty, clarity, grace. If it were a voice, it would be Donald Duck's. At its worst, it is simply illegible. It's the graphological equivalent of a lost breakfast. Because Arthur has a passion for neatness, he wishes it were tidier, better groomed, but his primary objection has to do with what he suspects it implies about him psychologically. Like most people, Arthur is inclined to believe that some small portion of a person's character is revealed in his handwriting. Handwritings, like fingerprints, are unique—no two are identical. Each says something about the person responsible for it. It doesn't seem likely that the mess Arthur makes could be saying anything about him that he would care to hear.

Like most kids, Arthur perfected his scribble in school. Armed with a fat red pencil and a large sheet of coarse, wide-ruled paper, he made a mockery of something called the Palmer Method. Like everyone else, Arthur practiced loops and ligatures until he was sick of them. His work was consistently bad—his ascenders absurd, his descenders hopelessly catawampus—but because he was a male, no one seemed to particularly care. Arthur may have been expected to write decently—he can't remember— but truly good handwriting, that was something for girls. To write nicely, it was implicitly understood, was to fly in the face of biology—something few boys his age felt compelled to do.

The horrors of one's handwriting are accentuated, Arthur has noticed, by what he has come to think of as writing's cruelest invention—the fine-point pen. It emphasizes the scraggly and chaotic qualities of one's script. Arthur blames this instrument on accountants and their intricately crosshatched ledger sheets—as they have proliferated, so too have these pens. They are everywhere:

fine, extra-fine, extra-extra-fine—pens that could only be of interest to an acupuncturist.

10

From a discarded short story titled "The Fax Machine":

We had a new director, a hyper-analytical, coffee-addicted, dressed-for-success guy with a terrible hyenaish sort of laugh that shocked you no matter how many times you heard it. He created a new position and filled it with a friend from his shady past—a man named Ross Tobolowsky. Ross, in turn, created his own new position—namely, assistant to himself—and filled it with someone he hoped would be a friend in the future: Jennifer Davis. She used to work in customer service. She was rumored to be adventurous.

11

From a discarded poem titled "Ice Cream":

What is it
but the felicitous
emulsification of psychiatry—
a scoop of cold security
on a sugar cone,
a spoonful of well-being,
a bowlful of therapy
with chocolate sauce. . . .

12

From a discarded short story titled "The Close-Up":

The man who is supposed to take my picture is a veteran of the fashion scene. He has long gray hair—like a lion's mane—which he combs back and goops in place so that it looks as if he's been caught, stop-action, staring into a gale-force wind. He has a signature style that trades heavily on the inherent drama of the black-and-white photo. He wants to make me look if not famous, at least significant— like someone from an earlier, more serious time. He poses me just off to the left of an ornately framed window, my chin up, my focus on posterity.

I don't like the finished product at all. I look grave and unhappy—like someone channeling Dostoyevsky or waiting in line at the post office.

13

From a discarded travel piece titled "Visa Las Vegas":

Our hotel is a small one just a block off the strip. It has tried to set itself apart from the crowd of other hotels in the area by focusing on the quality of its beds, which it describes everywhere in its literature as "world famous" and "heavenly." They are, I have to admit, nice beds—almost as nice as the extra-firm helipad I have at home. But does one really come to Las Vegas for this?

14

From a discarded poem titled "Computer":

> Though this tricked-up calculator
> of yesses and nos
> cannot ignore my persistent
> tapping on its shoulder,
> its daddy-like indifference to me
> is deep-seated and ineradicable.
> It suffers my syntax in silence
> and truly revels only
> in its own inexhaustible precision.

15

From a discarded short story titled "A Dip In The Jury Pool":

7:45 a.m. Check into Jury Assembly Room at the Washington County Courthouse. Don't really know what to expect. I have never actually been in court before. Embarrassing to admit, but most of my ideas about what our court system is—what it looks like, how it works—come from television. I can see immediately I am going to find little that is familiar.

The assembly room, for instance: it is completely devoid of the traditionally imposing, brown-tone ambience I have come to know and revere. Half-a-football-field long, it looks and feels very much like a bus station circa 1959. No hard-to-get taxpayer dollars squandered on elitist amenities. No marble, no walnut.

I am given a small handbook and a plastic ID badge to hang around my neck. I am juror 001763. There are more than two hundred of us here.

8:00 a.m. Orientation lasts almost an hour. We listen to three different speakers and watch a 15-minute video. It is basically your standard informative mélange with labored jokes inserted every so often like raisins in an oatmeal cookie.

Like everyone else, I am a seething cauldron of conflicted feelings. I am sort of proud to be doing my civic duty, to be providing a valuable public service whose importance to the maintenance of democracy is more precious than the right to vote (Thomas Jefferson), but I am unhappy about the disruption of my everyday life and concerned about missing too much work.

10:45 a.m. Have been eating granola bars out of my briefcase and reading a novel by Michael Frayn. I am on my third cup of really bad vending-machine coffee when the first group of names is called. Mine is not one of them.

16

From a discarded poem titled "John at Twenty-Four":

the cast-iron furnace drips
a scalding essence,
and the single gully
through which his every waking thought is washed
grows deeper, more cavernous,
until the tourists begin to gather—
drive up in their motor homes—

to gaze out at the grandeur of his banality
and spot, through an icy telescope
on the canyon's rim,
the seed of a pipsqueak soul
lost among the boulders.

17

From a discarded essay titled *"Patheticus Malidroitus Horticulturi"*:

Every so often, for reasons I don't fully understand, I feel compelled to try my hand again at house plants. There's just one problem: I have never been any good with house plants, and, judging from the evidence, it doesn't seem likely that I ever will be.

I am what is generally know in the trade as *patheticus malidroitus horticulturi*—or more colloquially, a guy with a brown thumb. Three weeks is about the longest I've ever kept anything alive.

18

From a discarded essay titled " Metcalf's Power":

The figures that populate Metcalf's paintings have a general tendency to be clothed (as opposed to the nudes of his drawings). If they are female—and most of them are—they are anachronistically gowned. They present a genteel formality that suggests everything from classical court paintings to contemporary scenes of the chiffon-centric Southern cotillion. They are emblematic, featureless figures who, with little more than position and posture, generate an impressive number of narrative possibilities.

But narration is not really what Metcalf's work is primarily about. These are modern paintings, and, as such, their central concern is with painting itself. While due consideration has been given to content, the real struggle is not with "story"—it is with form and facture, it is with the visual elements of painting. If we must say these pictures are about something, we must say they are about the orchestration of the dialogue both within and between the narrative and visual elements. The obsessional tinkering is about getting the music right.

19

From a soon-to-be-discarded poem titled "Drinks":

> I have spent my morning
> with a glass of milk,
> hiding from people
> who were taller than me;
> and my afternoon
> with a bottle of wine,
> lying to women
> about my immaculate intentions.
> I have spent my evening
> with a tumbler of antacid,
> trying to forget
> just a little of what I could not know;
> and my night

with a syringe of formaldehyde,
dying to fit myself
into the smallest and darkest of places.

THE VISIT

This is our special room. It's a nice place, comparatively speaking, for which we are expected to be thankful. That I am not thankful gets on some people's nerves, although it's not supposed to. Things like that—my thankless-ness—are supposed to be taken in stride, but some people here can't really take everything in stride that they're supposed to; they're offended, and, as a consequence, they often act unprofessionally towards me. That I am not a sufficiently thankful person is, I think, related to the question of why I am here, although I can't tell you exactly how. No doubt one of the grand inquisitors up-stairs has an idea—up there they have ideas about every-thing all the time.

My first two months here were no-visitor months, but I've been seeing her like almost once a week now for . . . well, I don't know how long.

Who have I been talking about . . . ?

Annette—that's who I'm talking about. That girl who says her name is Annette. I don't really know who she is. I mean, she's told me who she's supposed to be—who "we" are supposed to be—maybe half a dozen times, but I can't say I believe her. I have one of those deep-down-in-your-small-intestine feelings that she is working for Ba-cardi—that she is posing as this person, this "Annette," at his request.

For one thing, she seems way too comfortable in this building. A normal person—one who wasn't working for you know who— wouldn't seem comfortable at all. They would seem all tense and repulsed.

And there's another thing . . . there's the way she cocks her head when she's listening to you—it's not natural, it's . . . well, studied, rehearsed. It's the sort of head-cocking a professional person does when they want you to think they're taking a sincere interest in whatever it is you're saying.

It would be nice if she was who she says she is, but she isn't. I don't think she has any idea that I know that.

The last time I saw her, she brought me a whole armload of magazines.

She was watching TV, and there was this woman on who had written a book—some sort of "memoir" about growing up poor and unhappy in Tennessee—and she was saying how much writing about all that personal stuff had helped her, and she thought I might want to think about writing something . . . you know, about this place . . . about my experiences here. There are all sorts of essays in these magazines. She thought I might want to look at them and sort of get an idea of how it's done. It could be a project.

She portrayed this "project" as being something that might be good for me, but it was easy to see it was something Dr. Bacardi thought might be good for him. If I wrote something about this place it would be combed by all sorts of people for revelations, and those revelations would be noted in my file, and then some afternoon when I wasn't expecting it, when I was talking about my early interest in X or in Y, the good doctor would allude obliquely to one of them and try to catch me in some sort of defining behavior.

I told her I would have to think about it.

Along with the magazines, she brought me this plastic container with this blue bow taped to the lid. It looked like a regular sort of gift, but I could tell it wasn't really. I could tell it was a test—a test disguised as a gift.

Thanks.

It—the container—was filled with individually wrapped hard candies. They were all different shapes, and sizes, and colors—each, I am sure, with its own special psychometric significance. I couldn't be certain what I would be saying with my choice—you know, the red cylinder as opposed to yellow rectangle as opposed to orange square—so I decided to "invalidate" the message I was sending by purposefully choosing the piece I was least inclined toward. The green triangle, of course.

I had a little trouble getting the wrapper off this piece—it was one of those where the cellophane had gotten all fused with the candy somewhere in the manufacturing/wrapping process—and "Annette" offered to help.

She tried not to make it look easy, but I could see it was. I didn't really mind though. I could see what was involved.

What, some sort of elementary problem-solving ability?

No. It was fingernails.

Let me help you with that.

I could have done it, you know, but I don't have any fingernails. For all sorts of reasons—that I am sure you can imagine—they don't allow us to have fingernails.

In addition to the candies and the magazines, she likes to bring me these little stories of the world outside.

There was a story about a one-eared cat; and there was one about somebody's older brother who climbed some mountain in Africa and died of an edema during the descent; and . . .

Did I tell you about our office lunch? We went to Pagoli's. I think there were like ten of us. Janet, as usual, couldn't decide what she wanted and was driving everyone nuts. Anyway, there was a new waitress and somehow our orders got all mixed up and nobody knew what they were having. When the bill came it was impossible to understand so Leanna from accounting pulled an eyebrow pencil out of her purse and sorted it all out for everyone on a napkin . . .

I never believe any of these stories, no matter how carefully crafted or stuffed with picturesque detail. They're transparently part of her cover—concoctions designed to lend a certain credibility to the character of "Annette."

Of course, she always wants to know about my visits with Dr. Bacardi. How did they go? What did he say? What did I say? I have no idea what she is revealing to whom, so I always try to be very careful. I try to keep my exposures to a minimum. I know they are expecting me to say certain indicative things, and that these things can be accumulated and put in a report, and that—if necessary—this report can be used in legal ways to keep me here. No one has any real interest in my being released. There's the insurance money, and I am, I know—although he won't admit it—the subject of one of Dr. Bacardi's studies.

He wants to be famous you know. He wants to be asked to do a five-part series for the Public Broadcasting System where he will be flown to cities around the world to interview doctors and patients in various exotic therapeutic settings.

Tick tock, tick tock, tick tock, I can hear her coming—I can hear the clap, clap, clap of her hard-heeled shoes. As usual, I have started making a list of the things I am not going to talk about. I am not going to talk about stealing a trombone from the music room, or having certain fantasies, or about the drawing I made of an influencing machine, or about last night when I had that feeling again, the one I get all the time, the feeling that something not very good is going to happen.

I have no idea exactly what this something-not-very-good might be, only that whatever it is, it will be very much so. I tried to stay awake and on guard, but, of course, I couldn't. I fell asleep at my usual hour and had lots of strange mathematical sorts of dreams, which I didn't understand because I am not a mathematical sort of person. I suspect they were induced by the medication that is being surreptitiously administered here—in the form of a vapor—while we sleep. Anyway, whatever it is I feel is going to happen doesn't seem to have happened yet, but it's going to, I can tell you that. And something else I can tell you: when it does happen, there won't be anybody around here who can honestly say I tried to warn them, and for that I think you can blame Dr. Bacardi completely.

So, how have you been?

I've been fine. Fine, fine, fine, fine, fine.

Fine?

Yeh. Fine.

You don't look fine.

Is that what you're going to tell Bacardi?

What?

Is that what you're going to tell Dr. Barcardi—that I don't look so good.

David . . . what . . . what . . . what can I do for you? I've done everything I can think of . . . what can I do for you . . . .

What can I do for you . . . what can I do for you.

ANDREA AND LYNN
(A Situation Comedy)

1. WHERE IS ANDREA, AND WHAT IS SHE DOING?

Andrea is sitting at the dining-room table, her hair tucked behind her ears. She is in a mood. She is reading, as best she can, the shiny sheet of instructions she has just plucked from a just-purchased home-pregnancy test. A piece of origami, she has it unfolded and spread out in front of her like a map. The thing itself, the thing she is being instructed how to use, is sitting off to her left behind a cup of coffee. It is medical-looking and made of high-impact plastic. Its shape reminds her of the tire gauge that is at this very moment lost in the glove compartment of her car.

As she browses the highlighted section of these instructions, the section titled "Frequently Asked Questions" (How does it work? Do I have to test in the morning? What if the results. . .?), Andrea listens to Lynn who is on the phone with her sister Jean in St. Louis. Given the economical use of space in this apartment, listening to Lynn is easy as she is less than twenty feet away. She is draped bonelessly over the lower half of the livingroom couch, like something melted.

2. WHAT ARE LYNN AND JEAN DOING?

Lynn and her sister are arguing as always. This evening it started out about Dave, Jean's husband, a foul-mouthed software salesman with a too-tidily trimmed beard. He has apparently just finished an affair, and now, monogamous again for the first time in two years, has become more insufferable than usual, swollen up with a new-found sense of virtue. Jean is complaining about him in general, but she is specifically aggrieved about something he said to her the other night in front of everybody at their neighbor's famously boring end-of-summer party. Lynn is not sympathetic—she does not like Dave. She says the remark (which Andrea cannot quite catch, but understands to be some not-so-subtle allusion to Jean's persistent weight problem) is a typically Dave-type one, nothing that should surprise anyone.

3. WHERE DID THE ARGUMENT GO FROM THERE?

From Dave, the argument evolves, as it often does, into one about Andrea in which Jean suggests for the umpteenth time—via some transparent hypothetical—that she is a bad influence, and Lynn replies for the umpteenth time saying something to the effect that "Well, Jean, you're going to understand what you're going to understand."

As they move from subject to subject—their mother's lots-of-white-marble remodel of the downstairs bathroom (which Jean finds elegant, Lynn gaudy), to their father's rebound from a four-month-ago double bypass, to the ancient family Dalmatian's trouble with flatulence—Andrea notices Lynn does not mention the prospective child. It is easy to guess why. Jean has two children of her own, Frick and Frack, who she thinks are perfect (Andrea met them Thanksgiving and found them to be monstrous little ovens of ego, insatiable demanders of undivided attention). Lynn says nothing about being a possible impregnatee because she does not want a lot of Jeanish advice on the subject.

4. WHERE DID LYNN AND ANDREA MEET?

They met where you might expect—in a bar, a place called Shelley's. Andrea was there with a horrible, mean-spirited, simianesqe little person named Teresa, who she was seeing as part of some misguided effort to punish herself for the way she had behaved in a previous relationship.

She had just had a fling with the flu (she stayed home from work wrapped up in a cotton blanket like a burrito, watching television until her brain hurt), and she had not really wanted to go out but she allowed herself to be talked into it. Shelley's was supposed to be an evening celebrating her return to normal function. Although her head was still stuffed with steel wool and her spirit haunted by the hallucinatory scent of herbed cough drops, she was trying to make the best of it.

5. WHAT HAPPENED?

The celebration, such as it was, quickly foundered when, following a brief, post-sickbed high, Andrea fell into a typical pattern with Teresa of senseless sniping. She turned a simple, innocuous disagreement about the voice of the woman singing with the band (Andrea said she did not so much hit certain notes as scrape them) into a fully fledged pissing-off tiff. She admits now that her remark was not completely innocent, knowing as she did Teresa's sensitivity on the subject of voices (Teresa herself having a terrible one).

While in this instance Andrea was clearly the begetter of the discord, she was, nonetheless, the one who decided to stare off malevolently into the distance. It was while she was doing this staring-off that she made eye contact with a stranger two tables away. It was Lynn.

6. WHAT WAS LYNN DOING?

She was with a group of friends who seemed to be having a sort of prototypical good time. They were laughing, rocking in their chairs, and occasionally they threw their arms up in the air like they were on a roller coaster and had just taken a vertiginous plunge. Normally Andrea was put off by such aggregations of extroverts, but for some reason she was not this night. Several people in the group were what you would call structurally attractive, but for Andrea it was Lynn who stood out. Smallish, blonde—she had those milk-fed, just-bathed good looks for which Andrea was a complete sucker.

Lynn smiled. Andrea smiled. One thing, as they say, led to another. Three months later Lynn was moving in.

7. LYNN MOVES IN

Lynn was Andrea's third roommate in the past five years. Before her there was Carol, and before Carol there was Samantha—stories for another time.

She showed up at Andrea's place on the appointed morning in a rented van, an off-orange thing the color of tomato soup. "Well, here I am," she said. Andrea was impressed by both the quality and the quantity of her personal stuff. As a budding businesswoman (she owns "Andrea's," a small coffee shop inside Penrose Books downtown near the campus of Skidmore College where, as it just so happens,

Lynn works as a secretary in administration), Andrea was putting most of her discretionary income back into the business where Lynn had obviously been investing heavily in her wardrobe. She had a weakness for shoes and sweaters. When everything was out of the van, in the apartment, and in what was ostensibly its place, Andrea made a suggestion that surprised even her a little—namely, that sweaty and sore-backed though they were, they should conclude this day of drudgery not by relaxing out on the balcony with cokes, but with a good cleaning up.

8. GETTING TO KNOW ONE ANOTHER

Slowly they set about the complex and frequently tedious task of getting to know one another. As neither of them were especially gifted in this regard (they were not people who easily drew others out), things proceeded at what was probably a slower than average pace, but in eight months they had come a respectable distance. Many things were discovered—who liked to take a shower when, which vegetables were preferred and which were verboten, how long was too long to leave a pair of jeans on the closet floor—but there were still many mysteries to be revealed. Lynn, for instance, still had no idea that in high school Andrea had been a heavy user of recreational drugs. And Andrea, well she never in a million years would have guessed that Lynn, at the age of twenty-five, was thinking about a baby.

9. WHEN AND WHERE DID ANDREA FIRST DISCOVER LYNN'S INTEREST IN HAVING A CHILD?

They were in the car on the way to a much-despised aerobics class at the YMCA when from out of the proverbial blue Lynn brought up the subject. She said it was something she had been thinking about for some time and that she had decided it was something she wanted to do. Andrea was struck dumb, several different reactions colliding at an unmarked synaptic intersection deep behind her sinuses.

10. WHAT WERE THOSE REACTIONS?

She was hurt that their present life, unfolding voluptuously as it was, was not enough. Hurt that the decision that had been made had been made unilaterally, that her feelings had not been taken into consideration. (It was widely known that Andrea did not much care for children herself.)

11. AND?

She was angry.

12. AND?

She was fearful. Fearful of what introducing such a life-altering item into the present situation would do to that situation, what the assumption of a seemingly unassumable responsibility would do to their progressing, much-valued, mutual inclination to assume further responsibility for one another.

13. LYNN HAS A PLAN

Lynn described in detail a plan she had concocted whereby a baby-begetting might be brought to pass. She was determined to circumvent all the troublesome claims—present and future (legal and otherwise)—of paternity. It was absurd, goofy, simple-minded, cartoonish—the product of a mind reared on television. Andrea could not in any real sense "believe" she was serious, but she was.

As she drove along, she elaborated, her face, lit from beneath (by the dashboard lights), taking on a ghoulish blue hue. She said that as she understood this overwhelming desire of hers, it was simply a coming to fruition of the species' most basic urge: to reproduce. Andrea was suspicious. She felt certain this "understanding" was the work of a psychologist Lynn had been seeing—a very conventional, very bucktoothed woman named Blakely.

"Sounds like Dr. B talking," Andrea said.

"I suppose," Lynn said, flipping on the turn signal. "I mean, she has been helping me work it out--you know, emotionally."

14. ANDREA ASKED LYNN TO RECONSIDER

In a fumbling way, Andrea asked Lynn to reconsider. She thought introducing a bouncing baby uncertainty into the complex little system they called their relationship would be a mistake. Lynn said her mind was made up. Andrea said nothing. She felt like a cored apple.

15. LYNN CHOSE A PROGENITOR

Lynn chose the prospective progenitor quickly, her position as trusted secretary in administration at Skidmore making things easier than they might otherwise have been. She read capsule bios of the faculty in the back of the school bulletin, and, as if shopping from a mail-order catalogue, selected the ten most promising whose toast-colored files she surreptitiously pulled and read from cover to cover in the course of a week--fifteen minutes here, twenty minutes there—hidden in an out-of-the-way storage room, seated on an old, ergonomically incorrect typing table behind a phalanx of battered bookcases. It was a toss-up between a perfectly presentable man in the English Department, a quixotic explicator of postmodernist fiction, and the crown jewel of the Physics Department—the widely published, much honorarily-degreed, slightly hydrocephalic Dr. H. H. Hilderbrandt. She chose Hilderbrandt. Andrea was nonplussed. She did not want to fight Lynn about it--at the time, as part of a semi-silent protest of the whole project, she was trying to follow the path of least apparent involvement—but she was appalled. Physically HHH was so spectacularly unattractive that Andrea would have thought him automatically ruled ineligible. (She could see a big-headed, beetle-browed, HHH-resembling spawn, and it made her shiver.) Andrea herself grew up very plain-looking and was sensitive in a way Lynn could not be to the role such things as big ears and/or bugged-out eyes played in the development of personality—what was augured in the way of prospects for future happiness. But Lynn was enamored of the doctor's whopping IQ and was convinced his physiognomical misfortune could be mediated by what she modestly referred to as her own more regular features.

"But what if they aren't," Andrea asked.

"You're such a worrier," Lynn said.

16. DR. HILDERBRANDT

The seduction was ludicrously simple, like shooting middle-aged fish in a barrel.

Lynn went to Dr. Hilderbrandt's office on a trumped-up administrative errand—some sort of check of enrollment lists. She found the doctor hunched over his desk working on a speech he was scheduled to give in a week to a convention of eggheads in San Diego. His broad brow wrinkled like a sheet of cheap cellophane, he was trying to shoehorn a few jokes into a refurbished old stump shtick called "The Quantum Foam, A Point about Points." (With a sense of waning power—"no more fireworks"—HHH had given up "serious" scientific work more than a decade ago.)

Lynn walked up and tapped the doctor's office door— tap, tap, tap. Exercising the prerogative of genius to be unreceptive, HHH was about to wave her away, but when he looked up from the scribbled-over legal pad in front of him and saw Lynn in her Jack-the-Giant-Killer miniskirt, he stopped the about-to-be-executed dismissive wave and put his vast flow of ideas on hold.

17. LYNN INTRODUCED HERSELF

Lynn introduced herself and her bogus errand, and, while the good doctor was rutting around in one pile of computer printouts after another looking for the official enrollment record, she made a clever crack about the "chaotic" state of his office. Dr. H laughed and told her a long involved story about the first time he ever saw Einstein's famous office at the Institute for Advanced Studies.

They chatted for half an hour, Lynn pretending to be caught off guard by the doctor's wit and charm. That she seemed interested did not strike him as being in the least bit unusual. Eventually he invited her for a drink at the Lamplight after his afternoon seminar.

"That would be nice," Lynn said.

18. THE LAMPLIGHT

The Lamplight is a hovel, but it is near the campus

and is popular with the artsy-fartsy crowd as it is rumored to be the favorite hangout of Portland's presently famous outre filmmaker. It is paneled with over-varnished pine.

When they arrived, Lynn was laughing a little too insistently. They found a booth. Dr. H sat under a poster for an R & B band called Hiatus. The band was fronted by a portly harmonica player named Paul Hinder, a man Andrea's father once defended (unsuccessfully) on a cocaine possession charge. Lynn told one of her usual opening stories, the one about Boots, a dog from her childhood who would not eat sauerkraut, and Dr. Hilderbrandt responded with a long tale about his early infatuation with rocketry.

Everything was going well until, out of a pack of new arrivals, Michelle appeared.

Michelle is a masculine-looking person with a flattop and a small gold stud in her nose. She is Lynn's ex-inamorata. She walked over, said hello, and, in a winking way, asked Lynn who Dr. H was. Lynn thought her project was about to be scuttled. She introduced the two. Michelle was about to say something but suddenly stopped, having picked up the message from the tense way Lynn was acting that she had stepped into the middle of something she didn't fully understand. With a quick shift of gears, she graciously excused herself. One thing was clear: whatever Dr. Hilderbrandt might understand about the second law of thermodynamics, he knew nothing about lesbians. The only thing he said to Lynn following this encounter was "What an odd girl."

19. LYNN AND DR. H LEAVE THE LAMPLIGHT

When they were leaving the Lamplight the good doctor asked Lynn if she would like to go to dinner sometime. She lied and told him she was a good cook—why not come to her place?

"When?"

She said she would have to check her calendar. Dr. H thought she was talking about her social calendar, but she was, in fact, talking about her biological one. She told him she would call.

20. CHOOSING THE SEDUCTION MENU

As part of a too-little-too-late effort to make Andrea feel included, Lynn asked her to help with the seduction menu. At first she said no, but Lynn wheedled in that special way of hers and wimp-willed Andrea waffled, then agreed.

They sat down with a half-dozen cookbooks they borrowed for the occasion from a woman upstairs on nine, the wife of a restaurant critic who writes for a local weekly under the nom de plume of Mr. Dishing It Out.

Choosing the menu was easy as they agreed on the basic criteria: it should be simple, light, and aphrodisiacal. They had a good time—they were more like conspirators than cooks. They chose a pea salad, chicken wings with oyster sauce, and chocolate mousse.

21. WHAT SORT OF MUSIC DID ANDREA THINK HHH WOULD LIKE?

Lynn also wanted Andrea's help with the seduction music. What did she think HHH would like? Andrea guessed something highly numerical—baroque, perhaps Bach. But neither of them liked Bach. They found him insufficiently romantic and slightly nervous-making. They settled on a collection of fruity flute nocturnes by blarneymeister James Galway.

22. THE FATEFUL NIGHT

The fateful night arrived. Lynn was dressed in black gabardines and a tight white sweater. She was not wearing a bra. Andrea got kicked out. (She went down the street to Peggy Johnson's pathetic apartment in the moldy old Shamrock where Peggy and she watched the same movie they always watched when, for one reason or another, Andrea was visiting: *Dr. Zhivago*.)

Things went just as planned. Dr. Hilderbrandt arrived at seven on the dot. He was toting a flagon of expensive white wine and wearing a multicolored bow tie that bobbed at his throat like a manic bat. He greeted Lynn with a perfunctory kiss on the cheek. They toasted each other in the kitchen as Lynn put the finishing touches on the oyster sauce. Although she didn't really need the great man's help, she asked for it.

23. DINNER WAS A SUCCESS

Dinner was a success. There was considerable noise, much lip-smacking and um-umming, for the good doctor's table manners were those of someone who frequently ate alone. Lynn pretended not to notice, and when she felt a frown forming in the midst of one particularly gauche event, she turned it as quickly as she could into something resembling a motherly look of approval—something suggesting that nothing gave her more pleasure than to hear a good slurp, that she regarded this as the universal sign of a healthy appetite and a healthy appetite as the universal sign of a good character.

The chicken wings reminded Dr. H of Paris. He had been at an international physics conference and had eaten something very much like them there. He told Lynn about a woman he met at a pre-conference cocktail party—he couldn't remember her name, only that she was very unattractive and that she had been Ernest Hemingway's landlady at one time in the twenties when her circumstances were temporality reduced.

24. DR. H TOLD LYNN THE MEAL WAS WONDERFUL

When they finished dinner they moved into the living-room for coffee and mousse. Galway was playing just audibly in the background. Dr. H told Lynn the meal was wonderful and Lynn, moving in close to him on the nubby blue couch, thanked him. She could tell he was trying to assess the situation, trying to establish in a mechanical fashion their present position, determine their direction and speed. He wanted to know where they were going and when they might be getting there. Lynn decided to help. She leaned over and gave Dr. H a tentative kiss on the lips. This was followed quickly by a second and a third. Hormones engaged, things began to escalate. Dr. H moved his hand up to Lynn's generally lovely left breast, and, as he did so, she noticed—of all things—his fingertips were slightly yellow. The chalk from a decade of emphatic scrawling of formulae on various blackboards was ground into his skin.

25. KISSES AND CONSUMMATION

There were a dozen or so more kisses when Lynn took matters into her own hands so to speak. Having calculated the optimal hour for insemination to be approximately ten, she unzipped Herr professor's baggy pants, fished out his unexceptional example, and gave it a quick little lick. Dr. H's stunning IQ dropped so fast he got dizzy. Lynn scooped a finger full of leftover mousse from a dessert cup and spread it over the end of him. In less than a minute, Dr. H was as dumb as a duck. He tried as gallantly as he could to bring up the subject of condoms, but Lynn, feigning the urgency of passion, told him enigmatically to "never mind." Sensing a moment of hesitation she sat back and pulled off her sweater. What was left of Dr. H's massive intellect could now be used as a doorstop. The coffee table was pushed back and an energetic consummation took place on the floor in front of the couch. Lynn got a small red rug-burn on her elbow.

26. ANDREA NOTICED THE TIME

As Lynn and her sister Jean are comparing opinions about low-fat vs. no-fat dairy products, Andrea notices the time. It is almost nine. There is a show on TV she always watches, a maddeningly lackadaisical weekly news summary on PBS called, simply enough, The Sunday Evening News Hour. It stars a man named Carl Summers. In his mid-forties, blond-gray, overweight—he is the avuncular, quintessentially amiable presenter of the world according to the averagest of average Americans. It is a chance to compare visions, which, like the counterproductive inclination to let one's tongue play with an aching tooth, she cannot pass up.

Andrea refolds the instructions to the pregnancy test as best she can, and she makes a note to herself on a napkin to call the library reference line. Lynn and she have done their homework. They have read the latest studies in the New England Journal of Medicine that say the greatest probability of conception occurs during a six-day period ending on the day of ovulation. What Andrea

wants to see are the numbers if they exist—the odds under optimal circumstances of impregnation from a single
act of intercourse and/or the average number of such
acts required under optimal circumstances to produce a
single pregnancy.

As she turns to give Lynn the sign that it is time to get
off the phone, Andrea is stopped cold by a special gleam
of triumph she notices for the first time in Lynn's pretty
blue eyes. Although she is in the middle of a disagreement with Jean about the wisdom of ever wearing strap-
less dresses, Andrea can tell by the light in her apple-pie
face (it glows from behind her usual scrim of dusty-rose
foundation like a candle in a paper bag) that she is happy.
That moment when she announced her intention of having a baby—like a split-second driving error that sends
you through a guardrail and over a cliff—changed everything. It is the dime on which Lynn turned from whoever
she was into someone full of hope living a major part
of her life in the future, and Andrea from whoever she
was into someone full of despair living a major part of
her life in the past. What Lynn saw as the beginning of a
new life, Andrea saw as the end of an old. Andrea knew
in that moment what she would not or could not admit
until now—that even though it was not finished between
them, it was over.

Cradling the phone in the crook of her pretty neck,
Lynn looks up. Andrea's eyes fill with tears as she points
at the watch she is wearing, a small thing with a met-
al band that is wrapped tightly around her wrist like a
shackle.

THE PARADE
(A Bedtime Story)

My name is Peter Newley. I am a thirty-two year old defense analyst, troubleshooter, bureaucrat-about-town, and, as always, I was early. I have a fetish about punctuality that derives mainly from petty neurosis and the preposterous, albeit generous, notion that other people's time might be as valuable to them as mine is to me. If I sound a little cranky on the subject, it's because I am.

The office I was standing in belonged to Dr. Kasper Hook. It was one of the nicest in the building. Medium-sized, lined with serious walnut bookcases, it was perched significantly on the eighth floor. I say "significantly" because this building, which houses the preponderance of our Defense Department, has ten floors, and, as is so often the case with such institutional edifices, where you sit in it physically is directly related to where you sit in it organizationally. The farther you are from the ground, the farther you are from the groundlings.

As I was waiting for Dr. Hook, I stood looking out the window that was directly across from his desk. It faced our sprawling and much esteemed Veteran's Square. I watched the seamless stream of traffic below. It was an overcast, charcoal-gray morning. The cars, busses, and trucks had their lights turned on. In the intermingling circles they traveled, they looked like a jumble of cheap necklaces.

114

The door opened behind me. "Ah. Good morning, Peter. What seems to be going on in the real world this morning?"

Short, perfectly egg-shaped, Kasper Hook was in his mid-fifties. His head, which was formidable, seemed almost as large as his torso and was topped with a tall, stiff brush of bright white hair. He had the face of a basset hound. By sheer force of intellect and will, he had become an important man in a government he never took too seriously. He was an adviser to the Chief of Military Operations, and I was his principal aide—the most favored of four. We were here this morning for a committee meeting. The subject was our annual October Day Parade—that hallowed occasion on which we massed our might as best we could and marched it down Independence Boulevard for all to see—especially the Belgravians, our belligerent neighbors to the north. As a simple display of sovereign prowess, I don't suppose it was much by international standards—it was nothing compared to the Russians, for example—but when things went well (and they usually did), it invariably made our most cherished adversaries nervous, and, of course, that was all we could ever really ask. Kasper's inquiry as to the state of the real world implied what was obvious from his dilapidated appearance. Slightly frazzled, his drooping face drooping even more, his eyes red, his arms full of files and memoranda, he had spent the night researching something in the dungeon of documents below.

"You know," he smiled, "I think I've found an answer to the Malicott problem."

*

The Malicott problem Kasper referred to was Alexis Malicott, dignitary observer from Belgravia, the afore-mentioned belligerent neighbor to the north. Our president—a large man with relatively primitive propensities and a tendency to braggodocio indigenous to the species—had, in a moment of memorable bravado and bombast, invited the honorable Mr. Malicott to be an official guest at the parade. He would be welcome to observe first-hand from the reviewing stand with the president himself. Mr. Malicott accepted, of course, and therein lay the problem: a very impressive parade was ordered and a less than impressive one was available. For a number of reasons either too complicated, too secret, or too banal to go into, our procurement of noteworthy new weapons systems had not gone as well this year as we had all led one another to believe nor had our maintenance of old weapon systems been as good as it should have been. The problem was, as Kasper put it, "one of ends and means. We have an end in mind: we would like to stagger Mr. Malicott, but we don't have the means." The meeting we were about to have, like the meetings we'd been having these past three weeks, was to decide what to do about this.

*

Room H-811 was directly across the hall from Kasper's office. It was long and narrow like a coffin and was considered unlucky by a number of our more superstitious brethren. The walls ironically were a lily-livered green. They were festooned with tiring portraits, a Rogues' Gallery of unvaryingly gloomy national heroes. As part of some ill-advised strategy to make them look as large and legendary as possible, they had been teased, both the living and the dead, into solemn, almost snarling poses. Instead of looking serious and heroic, they had ended up looking only unhappy. There wasn't so much as a single twinkle in forty eyes. In the center of the room was a long, narrow, felt-topped table, and it was around this that we gathered. At one end, in the obvious position of prestige, sat General Leonard Brickstone, the Chief of Military Operations—a broad, bald, eyebrowless man with a passion for expensive sports cars and a tendency to indulge his temper. Along either side of the table sat the advisors, each with one aide. Kasper and I sat on the left-hand side, in the middle, between Dr. Macy and Dr. Zachery. "Shall we begin?" asked General Brickstone. "I believe when we last adjourned we were about to hear further from Dr. Novak."

As the discussion evolved, three distinct positions had blossomed, each with a group of advocates and a group of detractors. Kasper, unhappy with all of them, had so far abstained. The first suggestion was that we essentially do nothing—that we paint and polish the weapons we had and let it go at that. While it was, strictly speaking, a sensible suggestion, it did little for Dr. Zachery's reputation as he was the one who made it and who, with diminishing enthusiasm, was still championing it. Doing nothing, while popular in practice, is rarely popular in policy. It suggests a lack of application and implicitly casts aspersions on the cherished idea that all endeavor, be it ever so humble, is efficacious.

The second position involved a series of delicate diplomatic moves whereby Mr. Malicott was subtly, but explicitly dis-invited. This was the position supported by Dr. Valis and Dr. Bloch. The third and preeminent position, the position most zealously advanced, involved simple deception. As put forth by Dr. Novak and Dr. Macy, numerous counterfeit additions would be made and mingled with our arsenal. A battalion of artists and craftsmen would be conscripted to build cardboard cannons, wooden tanks, and papier-mâché missiles. "It would be astonishingly easy to build up the appearance of our forces with these counterfeit weapons," said Dr. Novak. "With a concentrated effort, we have time to increase our apparent strength by as much as twenty-five percent."

It was here that Kasper, flipping open one of his dog-eared files, interrupted. "Excuse me, General Brickstone," his voice deep and rolling as always, "I should say, before we go very much farther with this, that while I think Dr. Novak's proposal typically interesting, it has a serious, albeit pedantic problem. It is an improvement on Dr. Valis's plan, which, of course, was an improvement on Dr. Zachery's plan, but one thing in particular bothers me—sound. What sort of sound will these counterfeit weapons of Dr. Novak's make? It is one thing to set up wooden tanks to be surreptitiously photographed from a distance—it is something else to drive one right under someone's nose. How will it be propelled, and what will it sound like? These are important and, at the present, unaddressed questions." He paused for a moment to let Dr. Novak madden without distraction. Kasper and Dr. Novak had been antagonists ever since arriving in the department. They had grown to dislike each other intensely—a fact that neither of them took even the slightest pains to hide. "I have, I think, stumbled on a solution," he resumed. "It will cost us nothing, and it can increase our apparent strength by any percentage we wish——although I think for the sake of credibility, we should not increase it by more than fifty percent." He proceeded to make his proposal, which was wonderful in its simplicity. It got everyone but Dr. Novak's enthusiastic approval and was speedily adopted by a delighted General Brickstone.

Tanks were our primary concern. We wanted Mr. Malicott, et al., to head dejectedly back home thinking we had a lot more of everything than we did, but we were especially interested in getting him to reassess his government's estimates of our tank strength. If they thought we were putting time, money, and material into tanks, they would put time, money, and material into tanks. This was what we wanted as we had just finished developing, completely unbeknownst to them, a wonderfully effective new anti-tank missile. What Kasper proposed we do with almost everything in the parade, but especially with tanks, was to get as many of them operating as possible, drive them in front of Mr. Malicott and the reviewing stand—and then, when they were out of sight, circle them down Aviary Avenue and have them make another pass or two. It was inspired, and it was adopted.

*

Anton Dulick and I traded sly smiles. Anton was Dr. Knight's chief aide and probably my best friend in the department. A short, nervous man, he was bright, irreverent, and amusingly paranoiac. We were smiling because as things had worked out we were bureaucratic allies in this case, and Kasper's plan—now known as General Brickstone's plan—was working perfectly.

The day was similar to every other day of the past month in that it was overcast and drizzly. This we took as a providential sign because it was generally understood by those in a position to have such an opinion that there was no better sort of weather for displaying armaments. The overcast provided a light that was flattering, and wet steel, it was hypothesized, invariably appeared more menacing than dry steel.

Mr. Malicott, who was not more than ten feet from me, was busy being a serious yet convivial guest. With the balance of a gymnast he expressed polite appreciation without ever suggesting he was impressed—but it was obvious from certain facial mannerisms and by the expression that lurked behind that quasi-solemn, proper, respectful façade that there was a wonderful sense of alarm. Its presence was happily noted by all concerned.

The parade, which had lasted almost an hour and had featured four passes of our tanks with two passes each of our missiles and our artillery, was over a little before noon. Our troops were very impressive. We had quite a large number of them who did nothing but practice close-order drill, and they were very good at it. It was, as always, a little unnerving to see such a mass of armed men perform with such perfect synchronicity. It is unnatural and terrifying in its exemplification of single-minded resolve.

If there was any flaw in the morning's event, it had to do with the construction of the reviewing stand. It was small for the number of people we packed onto it. The collective weight of officialdom being what it was, it seemed strained to the limits of its capacity. Whenever anyone so much as shifted in his seat, the entire structure swayed. A concern for personal safety intruded on the festivities and occasionally distracted attention away from the spectacle.

"You know," Anton said, "if this stage doesn't collapse and kill everybody, it's going to be very nice to be Dr. Kasper Hook when this extravaganza is over."

It was also going to be very nice to be Dr. Kasper Hook's chief aide.

*

Zota's was a small, dark, woody bar just around the corner from our office building. It was a favored establishment because it was close and because the owner, a former defense department agent (aware of the more romantic workings of a defense department man's heart), had decorated it to look like a den of surreption. It was lit in such a way as to make everyone in it look suspicious. It made even the most common physiognomy appear interesting, so we took to it like ducks to water. It was always pleasant to pretend we were there on large, secret business when, in fact, we were in all likelihood only hiding from a churlish superior. I was there two days after the parade at the invitation of Carter Kersey, an aide of Dr. Zachery's.

Carter was something of an interdepartmental mascot. As an aide to Dr. Zachery, he had no hope of any sort of advancement. He was considered reconciled to this and, consequently, safe as a friend. Everyone liked him, and everyone confided in him. A truly phenomenal amount of information flowed through him. He was often sworn to secrecy, but those who insisted on this precaution did so at their own risk and knew it. Carter's oath was a sieve. We gambled, not knowing what he would withhold and what he wouldn't. It added adventure to the day. It was the price you paid for information about everyone else. When he called me and suggested a quick drink at Zota's, I knew something was up. It was invariably we who sought out Carter—it was almost never the other way around.

I was, of course, early. I had found a booth and ordered a glass of wine when Carter arrived.

"Hi Peter, " he said. "How are you? Am I late?"

"No, not at all."

Carter struggled to get out of his voluminous overcoat. "What are you having—anything interesting?"

"Not really—Spanish, oaky as usual."

We exchanged pleasantries until the demands of propriety had been fulfilled, and then Carter got to the point. "The parade really went well for you and Dr. Hook, didn't it."

"Yes, as a matter of fact it did. It went better than we expected."

"Rumor has it that Dr. Hook's influence with General Brickstone has increased and that the General is thinking about promoting him to the post of Special Adviser."

"Yes, we've been hearing something about that. Nothing definite. We've been trying to track it down and get something more specific, but we're not having much luck."

"Novak has heard the rumors too. He is, as you might imagine, a little upset. He thinks Hook's a bit flamboyant."

"He thinks anyone with an I.Q. two points above average is flamboyant."

"That's true," Carter said. "But you know, don't you, that Novak is fanatical?"

I sipped my wine.

"I have it on good authority that he and Dr. Macy are plotting against your man. I don't know exactly what they've planned, but I know it's serious and that it's got a few people worried about Novak's mental balance. It is supposed to be extreme."

I thanked Carter for the report. I told him not to worry, that we would look into it. I tried to repay him as best I could, but I was a little short of funds. Kasper had just discovered that Arthur Winston's wife, Mira (Winston was Dr. Bloch's chief aide), had consummated an infatuation with a young man by the name of Ted Glasheen, a minor administrator in National Finance. It wasn't much, especially in view of what he had just given me, but Carter appreciated the effort.

*

The wait to discover what Dr. Novak was up to was neither long nor tense. Both Kasper and I underestimated his envy and rancor. Kasper didn't seem at all worried, and I was only vaguely uneasy—the way you are when something is in the process of going wrong with your car.

A week after my drink with Carter, Dr. Novak made his move. It involved nothing less than the coarsest kind of treachery. It was the sort of thing I am always accusing people of being able to do without really believing it. When actually confronted, I was as shocked and nonplussed as the next guy.

I arrived at the office early as usual and found the building alive with activity. I ran into Kasper getting off the elevator. He looked concerned. He took me into his office. "I've had two meetings already this morning, and I am destined for many more," he said disconsolately. He showed me the source of the trouble, the cause of all this frowning and official hubbub. It was a newspaper—not our newspaper, but the Belgravian *Voice of the People*—Malicott's newspaper. There on the front page in the boldest headlines, "Famous October Day Parade A Hoax." The story, which seemed interminable, was a detailed account of our deceptions. Kasper was, he said, in serious trouble. His plan had backfired. We now seemed slightly ludicrous, possibly desperate to our enemies—our security was jeopardized, and Dr. Novak was leading a frenzied contingent that was blaming him.

*

Dismay spread over the department like syrup over a stack of pancakes. It affected everyone. It was presumed that Malicott, et al., had received their damaging information from spies—presumed by everyone that is but me, Kasper, and possibly Carter Kersey. We thought it was Novak. Eventually we knew it was Novak.

In the exhaustive investigation he was conducting as part of the parade postmortem, Kasper had discovered one of the most common and valuable commodities of any and all bureaucracies: a disgruntled clerk. His name was Felix Kincaid. He was employed in Macy's office and had had his character attacked and his self-image scuffed in numerous altercations with Macy's chief aide. On several occasions Felix had overheard Dr. Novak and Dr. Macy discussing the advisability of leaking information about the parade. He would swear to it.

Upon simple investigation, the tracks of Novak and Macy were easy to trace. However accomplished as analysts and advisers, they were the rankest amateurs as subversives. With little trouble, Kasper was able to discover that they had traveled separately under assumed names to a small hotel on the border where they had met with a mustachioed agent of Malicott's government. Over a dinner of lamb and eggplant, they had passed our state secrets. Several hotel clerks, it seems, could readily identify them.

*

Kasper had a difficult time getting a meeting called as he was anathema to most of the resident aspirants—carrying, as he was, the ignominious mark of disfavor. Characterizing it as a preview of the postmortem, he did, however, manage. It was top secret and for counselors only. "Wish me luck," he said as he started for the committee room with a file as fat as a phone book. Without a file, Kasper was formidable; with one, I always felt he was invincible. Wishing him luck was simply a formality.

The meeting lasted thirty minutes. Kasper emerged wearing the slightest of smiles; Dr. Novak and Dr. Macy emerged wearing square-jawed guards.

That evening I invited Kasper to Zota's for a drink. I ordered a bottle of moderately priced champagne. "To vindication," I said, popping the cork.

"I'm, of course, not going to pass up a drink, but I'm afraid we will have to change that toast. We have not been vindicated, although we have been, to some extent, revenged."

It was weeks before I realized exactly what he meant, but eventually it was depressingly clear. By simple association with the debacle, Kasper's name was devalued. The question of guilt, innocence, culpability didn't matter. It was a difficult truth, but one borne out by the evidence. There was, over a period of time, a steady and insidious diminution of Kasper's responsibilities. Finally there was reassignment to a small, primitive outpost and, in response, a resignation.

I, of course, was shuffled off to a lesser position with a new adviser—a man by the name of Fussell. He is decent enough, but he is unexceptional in every way. I can see the handwriting on the wall, but I don't think I am presently prepared to read it. The departmental druids are saying that before the year is out Fussell will be gone, and me with him. They are probably right. If I were just a touch more world-weary I would resign like Kasper and save just the smallest piece of personal dignity for my scrapbook. However, deep down where I store a bureaucrat's most cherished misconceptions, I cannot help but hope that eventually this won't be held against me. It is very difficult to believe that the black mark beside one's name has been made with an indelible pen. It makes life serious in the most unfunny way.

ABOUT THE AUTHOR

K. B. Dixon has published poems, stories, and essays in a number of journals. He has written visual arts reviews for *The Oregonian*, and he was, for a time, a regular columnist for both *Scene Magazine* and *Metro Magazine*. He lives in Portland, Oregon.

Printed in the United States
55696LVS00003B/28-105